LOVE BEYOND THE STORM

(Storm Warnings)

Emily Sedlacek Spitler

My mom, Emily Sedlacek Spitler, was an extraordinary woman. She was determined, hard-working, stubborn and creative. I also have those qualities and that is why this book is coming to fruition a year after her death.

She loved to read. For as long as I can remember, we always had a library in our house with walls of books. She always dreamt of writing a book. We always knew that her first book would be a cookbook but in the early 1990s, she started having a reoccurring dream. She would dream the same dream over and over until she would write it down. Then the story would continue the next night until she would write it down. Pretty soon, she had the beginning of what she would call "Storm Warnings". It would take her several years and several revisions until she decided that it was finished.

Those very few of us who were given a chance to read it were amazed and spellbound. But no publisher was interested in publishing a book that was written by a former businesswoman who owned her own knitting/craft store in small town Prague, Oklahoma that grew out of her love of knitting and crafts. That store, "The Knitting Needle" would eventually become "Emily's Gift World" when she added gift items & glassware. That lady would eventually join her husband in the real estate business as a broker and then go on to helping me run my dance studio and dancewear store. And then in the final two years of life, start another business called "Emily's Creations" designing and making stained glass mosaic artwork.

Mom would go on to write another book "Lord Love A Duck" which may be published. Or may not. Who knows. Both books would just sit on the shelves collecting dust. While going thru some keepsakes after her death, we found a folder. Written inside was the following:

"This book is based on favorite recipes used through four generations of my family -my mother, her mother before her, me and now, my daughter. Being of Czechoslovakian descent, we each have had pride and enjoyment in our cooking expertise."

So it looks like she was planning on publishing a cookbook afterall!

This past year has taught me many things. One of which is don't wait. We keep putting things off saying that we will get to it or we will save it for later. What if tomorrow never comes? Do it now. I am just sad that she never got to see her large mosaic mural masterpiece being sold. She never got her book published. So many things like that.

I am determined to change that for her. I know she is watching down upon me. So mom, I'm publishing this book for YOU. I have always seen this book as a movie - who knows if that will happen. And yes, I'm going to publish the cookbook too!

Her determined and stubborn daughter,
Stacey Spitler

Chapter 1

<u>It was a humble beginning for the tiny, delicate wispiness that was growing ever so slowly. Drawing strength into itself, it steadily became more ominous and dark—eerie--threatening...With splaying fingers stretching outward like dangerous flicks of flame, it never ceased to move as if--searching--seeking....</u>

"Yes. It is perfect," the young woman whispered, as she lingered in the open doorway of the charming white farmhouse. Amy's eyes, blue as the summer sky at which she was gazing, sparkled as she gazed ecstatically over the beauty and peacefulness surrounding her. Wrapped in a silken cocoon of euphoria, she watched the white wispy clouds drifting lazily across the horizon. Having feelings of bottomless peace and satisfaction, Amy was blissfully happy and full of life. Life for her couldn't have been more perfect than at that moment.

She didn't see what lay far beyond the horizon, growing--waiting--until it was time. For the present, she was kept innocent of the expectancy and foreboding drama that would come into play that would affect not only her life, but also the lives of those near her.

Amy breathed in the fresh country air, her senses alerted to the sights and sounds of the great outdoors. Carried through the air by the gentle breeze, the delightful fragrance caused her to smile in enjoyment and contentment.

The slender jean-clad woman, desiring more of this new-found ecstasy, stepped out onto the front porch of the farmhouse, and relaxed against a pillar.

Marveling over the beauty surrounding her, Amy wondered as she often did during these last few months of what would happen if it were all taken away from her and Matthew. She didn't think she would be able to stand losing this once she had found this happiness.

As far as Amy was concerned, she was happier than she had thought possible, but she wondered if this was going to be enough to make Matthew happy and content. This was exactly what he had always wanted and dreamed of. He had talked about living on a farm numerous times. Now that he had his wish, she felt he was driving himself far too much, never being satisfied in his efforts of improving their new home. She wanted him to be as content as she was with their lives.

Compared to what their lives had been before they moved to Kansas, leaving their lives in New York City behind them, she thought their lives could not be more perfect than it was now; however, the question remained if it would, or could, last. Could this farm save their marriage? Possibly she was somewhat paranoid that her plan wasn't going to work.

Will she awaken to find this to be only a dream? If it was only a dream, she didn't want to awaken. Not ever.

There was nothing different about today. It was simply another perfect day as far as Amy was concerned, like the day before, and the day before that…and like it will be tomorrow. It was a day like which she would want to last forever. Each day, being a new adventure to her, made her always eager to face the new day in anticipation.

She gazed with pride at her surroundings. Rambling roses of crimson and delicate pinks climbed along the porch railings that wrapped around two sides of the house. Enclosed within the white picket fence was the lush green expanse of the lawn bordered by an array of beauty.

Adorning the border were flaming azaleas, blushing hydrangeas, and old-fashioned purple lilacs, along with the fresh scent of evergreens placed to compliment the bright floral colors surrounding them. There were flowerbeds filled with colorful annuals. Tiny delicate flowers of the ageratum and delightful pansies graced the walk leading to the front porch.

A majestic maple stood in one corner of the yard, among other smaller trees. Beauty, peace, and tranquility reigned in this remote country surrounding.

She smiled. Amy had never before envisioned owning anything as beautiful as this. She was captivated by the beauty surrounding her, and in the thought that it was all theirs.

A gentle breeze whispered through the leaves of the magnificent trees that stretched their limbs to the blue sky above. Birds were tending to their young in unseen nests and songbirds were singing joyously. Sounds of the cicadas were evident during the late afternoon, soon to be followed by the songs of the crickets as they welcomed the night hours.

Amy listened to the sounds surrounding her. What could be more wonderful and more right? She was positive they made the right decision of coming to Kansas and making this their home. At times she missed the hustle and bustle of New York City where she had lived all her life, and being totally different from what she was accustomed. It was difficult at times to make the adjustments, but she was trying with her entire being to get accustomed to this new way of life. At times, she wondered if she could really do it.

She was determined enough to give it a try. She had to, if she was to save their marriage. So far, she had every hope that they could make it.

A faint fresh scent of paint from the house lingered in the air, giving the old house a new charm. She was quite pleased with the results of what they had achieved in restoring the estate within the six months since they had purchased it.

The old house had been in dire need of work. Even in the deteriorated state it was in, Amy and Matthew McCormack knew when they had seen this farm estate for the first time, they had come home.

#

"Jus' needs some cleanin' up. You'd be surprised what a little paint can do," the elderly realtor suggested, as he led Amy and Mathew on a tour of the deteriorating estate.

Without any family to speak of, Harry Deakins, a veteran of the real estate market, simply refused to retire from his work. He was satisfied and happy to occasionally sell a piece of real estate. Making him happiest was when he had a listener with whom to share his experiences.

Everyone he met enjoyed hearing the colorful stories about the places he had seen and the people he knew so well. Today was no exception. Harry and the house that stood before them enchanted the young couple tremendously.

His eyes clouding with visions of the past, Harry shook his head sadly, and continued his reminiscing, "I remember when this place was once a real showplace. I sure hate seein' it goin' to neglect. People who own it are both too old now to keep it up. He's in a nursin' home now, 'n' she can't take care of the place by herself. They sure do hate havin' to give up this old place."

On close inspection, Amy and Matthew saw that the property needed a considerable amount of repair. The eager young couple, however, visualized immediately the possibility of what they each could do to restore this unique place back to its natural beauty and charm.

Matthew and Amy observed that the house definitely needed a new roof, and that rotting wood left weakened spots in the porch floor, making it unsafe to walk upon.

"The paint is peeling in many places," Matthew said, "and would have to be repainted. And the house would definitely need a new roof."

"It would have to have a lot of work done to the yard, too," Amy said, observing the unkempt yard, as well as the surrounding grounds which were overgrown with weeds. The garden spot lay barren and dry.

As they toured the interior of the old house, they saw that it was in desperate need of a complete redecorating. With Amy's knowledge of interior decorating, she knew much work would be needed and that it would be well worth the effort...if it was theirs.

The wallpaper was faded and yellowed; patches of the peeling paper hung loosely in several corners, and the woodwork throughout the house needed refinishing.

Once outside again, they each got lost in their thoughts. They could see the exterior of the house in a glistening new coat of white paint. The white picket fence needed painting as well, along with the barn, silos, and other outbuildings. There were fences to be replaced and corrals to be mended.

"This will require a lot of work," Matthew said. "But, in all probability, we could do much of the work ourselves. Do you think you can handle a hammer?"

"Just give me one, and see for yourself," Amy answered laughingly as she challenged him.

Feeling confident that they could accomplish this task, he desired to take the challenge. There would be no hurry. They had the rest of their lives.

"What do you think, Amy? Shall we buy it?" Matthew asked, his sparkling eyes meeting those of his wife with eager anticipation. Seeing her nod her head in approval, he had to ask, "Amy, are you sure you want to do this?"

Matthew couldn't believe that this was actually happening. This was what he had always wanted and dreamed about...a farm in Kansas like he had once before. He remembered how happy he had been. Now it could become a reality.

"Yes. Oh, yes, let's do," Amy eagerly agreed as she met the gaze of her husband.

Suddenly, she had mixed feelings as confusing thoughts raced through her mind. She couldn't believe she had agreed. It was too absurd. She must have been out of her mind...They couldn't just pack up and move here. But, yet, why couldn't they? She knew, without a doubt, that Matthew and Chrissie would be happy here, so why not?

Amy's mind filled with ideas. She could see many possibilities of what she could do in redecorating the house and sprucing up the yard. They could make it a real showplace.

Amy clasped her hands together in ecstasy over what they would have to look forward to if this was theirs to own. Never before having the opportunity for such an undertaking, she looked forward to the challenge.

As she gazed around the yard area, she could visualize planting some roses...climbing roses would look beautiful there all along the porch railings. They could plant some shrubs. She could already see the flowering kind growing there. Along the fence would be an excellent place for shrubs. Lilacs! Oh, yes, lilacs...the sweet glorious fragrance of the old-fashioned purple lilacs would be ideal. She could almost smell their fragrance.

Amy came to a final decision. Her answer would undoubtedly be "yes". In her heart, she knew they would be doing the right thing by purchasing the old farm estate. Having made her decision, she became hopeful that they would now find the answers they needed in saving their marriage. It would be a fresh, new beginning for them, especially for Matthew, and it would be a wonderful place for Chrissie to grow up.

Chrissie will have a real yard to play in. Oh, she'll love it," Amy said, as she surveyed the white fenced yard that surrounded the charming old house, thinking about their daughter they left behind in New York City.

"Yes, she will indeed," Matthew answered. "I could make her a swing over there. I had one when I was a boy," he said, pointing to a low hanging limb of the maple tree in the corner of the yard. "I could build her a playhouse in the backyard, there by the--"

"Hey, wait a minute, Matt. She is only two years old. Isn't that a little young for a swing?" Amy asked, interrupting him, unable to keep from bursting out in laughter. Even though it was amusing, she thought it was a wonderful idea, even if their daughter was a bit small.

"Well, it doesn't hurt to think ahead, does it?" Matthew answered in defiance. "Besides, this clean fresh air will be good for her, and she'll love it. You wait and see."

"Oh, yes, Matt, it will be. It is a perfect place to raise a family. I can't believe there is this much room."

"Can't you just see our little girl turn into a real tomboy...dirt, sunburn, and all?" he said, teasing his wife in amusement, "And you, too. I can just picture you with 'farmer's arms'."

"What do you mean? What are farmer's arms?" Amy asked in puzzlement.

Matthew only smiled. Envisioning her cream-colored arms being sun-streaked gave him the sudden urge to slide his hand down her arm and tighten around her waist, and giving her a warm affectionate hug.

Responding to his gesture, Amy leaned into him, and said, "The air does smell so fresh. It's remarkable how quiet and peaceful it is here."

Amy was amazed how this peaceful country atmosphere differentiated from the large city in which they had lived. Comparing the farm estate that lay before them from their city lifestyle in New York, she felt confident in their decision to purchase the farm estate. She knew that Matthew and Chrissie would love living here, and she was certain she could adapt to this new lifestyle with little difficulty.

"If you like the quiet, you'll love it here. Nobody lives 'round here 'cept Lizzie Thornton...'cept a couple of neighbors farther down the road. Lizzie's got the place next to this one," Harry said, "over there." He gestured toward the unpainted gray stucco bungalow sitting on top of a grassy knoll.

Surrounding the small house were only a few straggly trees, looking as dismal as the house itself. A few feet from the house stood what remained of a tree which had been struck by lightning years ago, leaving a dead and weathered trunk, its top charred and ragged. A hawk perched lazily on a ragged point of the trunk awaiting some unsuspecting prey.

Amy and Matthew followed Harry's gaze. They were astonished that someone actually lived in that forlorn-looking house where there didn't appear to be any sign of life.

The scene before them gave Amy a slight apprehension. A cold chill traveled through her spine. Immediately chastening herself, she realized it was foolish and wrong to be affected in this way. She knew she was being unduly judgmental, for she didn't know anything whatsoever about the woman living next door. She knew, also, that she would have to accept the fact that this woman would be their new neighbor, and they would need neighbors here in the middle of nowhere.

Curiously, Amy took in every detail of the small, neglected house and surrounding grounds. She observed that there were plain white curtains billowing out a small open window. She felt that the contrast of the stark whiteness with the dismal surroundings seemed somehow out of character, causing her to shudder involuntarily.

"Does she live alone?" Amy asked.

"Yeah, doesn't have much to do with folks 'cept comes into town every once in a while, bringin' in her herbs to Farmer's Market," the older man confided. "Hasn't been the same since the accident."

"Accident?" Matthew asked. Interested in hearing more about Lizzie Thornton, he and Amy urged the older man to continue.

"What kind of accident was it? Please tell us about it," Amy asked.

"Yeah, 'bout forty years back, t'was, Lizzie's husband 'n' kid was killed in a car wreck on the way into town. Jus' down the road there, t'was," the elderly gentleman related while he stared off in the direction of where the tragic accident had taken place. "T'was over there at that intersection. They were hit head-on by a drunk driver. The old son-of-a-gun walked 'way with jus' some scratches 'n' bruises."

Harry, lost in his remembrance, continued sadly, "The kid was only 'bout five or six. Sure was a pretty lil' young'un. A shame... sure was a shame. Lizzie fairly near lost her mind, she did...Never been the same since."

Harry remembered the incident as if it had happened only yesterday. He had known Lizzie and Philip since the time they had been in school many years ago.

He remembered with clarity when the very popular Lizette Stern married Philip Thornton, which nearly broke his heart. He had hopes of winning the affections of the lovely dark-haired girl for himself, but she only had eyes for Philip. While Lizette and Philip were saying their wedding vows, Harry made his own vow. He vowed he would never love another woman as he loved her.

When Harry learned of the accident, he had hastened to Lizzie's side to console her. Afterwards, he always was ready to lend her a helping hand, but she had a mind of her own, and made it clear that she preferred to be left alone.

"Lizzie, I jus' wanna help," Harry pleaded.

"But I don't need, nor want your help. I'm doing just fine by myself."

"Well, okay," Harry answered. "If that's what you want, but will you please, at least, let me come by once in a while to see if you need anythin'? Believe me, Lizzie, it won't be any bother, 'n' I sure would feel lots better 'bout it if you would let me."

"Okay, Harry, if you insist, but, I'll be all right," Lizzie said, relenting to his request, but added, "I can take care of myself. I've been doing it for years."

"Thank you, Lizzie. That makes me feel much better."

Harry felt sad for Lizzie, knowing she was holding her grief silently inside of her, refusing to let go. He grieved for her, but he could do little to help her, except to stand by if she should ever need him. He lived for the day that she would be ready to look at him as someone more than a friend.

Breaking into Harry's thoughts, Amy pressed for further information about the elderly woman, as she asked, "Does this woman have any other family?" She wanted, as well as needed, to learn as much as she could about this mysterious woman she had never seen, and will soon be her new neighbor.

What they had been told about Lizzie Thornton should have satisfied Amy's curiosity, but it had only intensified her desire to hear more. Unfortunately, the more she learned about the old woman, the more uncomfortable she became.

Amy chastened herself again for letting her imagination take hold of her this way. She had to remember that the poor woman had obviously never gotten over her tragic loss. Amy couldn't help but think, nevertheless, that it was unusual that the woman still mourned after all these years.

"None that I know 'bout 'n' I don't think she's got any friends either," Harry, rousing from his reflections, answered. "I come by to check on her every once in 'while, what with her bein' 'lone, 'n' all."

"Oh, that is tragic. I know it is terrible to lose someone you love like that," Amy remarked, remembering the terrible loss she, herself, had suffered when she had lost both parents a few short years ago when they perished in a plane crash, leaving her alone until Matthew came into her life.

Trembling, she thought how she would feel if anything would happen to her husband and child. It was too unbearable to even think about.

"Folks pretty much leave her 'lone as, like I said, Lizzie doesn't like to be bothered. They think she is a bit off her rocker, but they jus' don't understand what she's been through, like I do."

"What does she do with her time since she is alone?" Amy asked out of curiosity.

"She grows herbs…dries them 'n' such. She makes some kind of tonic with 'em, too." With a coy smile, Harry added, "and she makes a pretty darn good dandelion wine, too."

Listening to Harry, Amy and Matthew were curious and eager to hear as much as they could. Not only did they want to hear more about their fascinating neighbor-to-be, but they desired to know more about entire neighborhood. Proud as a peacock to be helpful to the newcomers, Harry was more than happy to comply in telling them more.

Becoming hopeful, he thought maybe this young couple could be exactly what she needed…new neighbors close by, someone she can get acquainted with, and she would not be alone all the time.

After some time had passed, Harry realized that he was taking too much time talking. From experience in his real estate profession, he knew he should leave the young couple alone for a while to formulate their dreams.

Sighing wistfully, he thought about being young like them again, to have a future ahead, to be able to dream again, and to realize that dream. Within the depth of his heart, he knew that dream meant Lizzie Thornton.

"I've gotta get back to the office, folks. Feel free to look 'round to your liken'," Harry said.

"When you're ready, give me a call, 'n' we'll get the paperwork to rollin'. Then 'fore you know it, it'll be yours. It'll be nice to get a young couple like yourselves in there to fix it back up 'gain jus' like it's supposed to be. That's jus' what this place needs."

Harry Deakins, however, had his doubts about how much this young city couple knew about farm life, and if they knew anything involving the undertaking of a restoration as this place needed. He shook his head negatively, positive that they wouldn't be able to last.

Harry didn't know that this was a young man who was at last realizing his dream, and beside him was a determined woman who was going to do everything in her power to help him achieve it. Matthew's dream was now Amy's dream as well. Little did they know of the challenges they would have to face and to overcome before making their dream a reality.

Chapter 2

Amy, absorbed in her reflections, leaned against the white porch column. Closing her blue eyes, she lifted her lovely face to the cooling sensations of the fresh air, as a wavy blond tendril fell unnoticed across one eye. She took a long deep breath of the gentle breeze which caressed her skin and teased her shoulder-length hair.

A few moments later, Amy opened her eyes and scanned the surroundings around her. Her eyes swept over everything from the majestic oaks and the delicate maples down to the rich dark earth of the vegetable garden where tender green plants were growing taller with each passing day. She marveled at the beauty around her and wondered how she ever doubted what Matthew had described to her about the farm life that he had known so well.

She smiled as her eyes settled on her husband who was busy at his tasks in the barnyard. Watching him absorbed at what he loved to do, it made her feel they had made the right decision by coming to Kansas, even though this was such a different way of life from what she had known. She had taken a gamble, but it had been worth it.

Sighing with fulfillment, she returned her gaze to the landscaped yard before her. The intermingling scents of the rambling roses, the honeysuckle vines, and the blossom-filled lilac bush combined to make a delightful fragrance. The wonder of what she would have had to pay for just that "perfume" back at Saks Fifth Avenue brought a smile of pleasure to her lips.

Absorbed in her thoughts, Amy didn't notice her husband pause at his work in the barnyard. Drops of moisture clung to his forehead. Stabbing the prongs of the pitchfork into a mound of soft hay, Matthew wiped his brow with a handkerchief he pulled from his hip pocket. Matthew had been hard at labor spreading out new straw on the barnyard floor, and the late afternoon rays were warm upon his bronzed back and shoulders. Earlier, he had removed his blue shirt and tossed it onto a post of the corral railing. The cooling breeze brushing against his bare torso felt invigorating on his hot, damp skin.

Glancing toward the house, Matthew saw Amy leaning against the porch column, lost in her daydreams. A smile came to his lips as he breathed in the sight of his beloved wife standing on the porch dressed in her faded denim jeans and tailored shirt with rolled-up sleeves, which accentuated her slenderness. There was both delicacy and strength in her face. He thought she couldn't be more beautiful than at that moment.

His smile widened, thinking this was, without a doubt, quite different from the elegantly coiffured hairdos and silk blouses of a few months ago.

Matthew waved to get her attention, smiling with eyes full of a mischievous light that always became electric when he laughed.

Watching her, he couldn't resist the urge to call out to her saying, "Hey, pretty lady. What are you doing there? Idling your time away? I know of a few hogs that need slopping right now. Aren't you rather shirking your duties?"

Matthew's teasing words and laughter penetrated through Amy's thoughts when she heard his cheerful voice. Her face brightening into a broad smile, she matched his irresistible smile as she waved to him.

"You think you are being funny, but they were asking for you," she answered, barely able to keep the laughter from her voice, as she played along with him.

She knew he enjoyed teasing her about slopping swine even though didn't own any. She grimaced at the thought of the dirty animals, and she was quite glad there were none on their property. In spite of herself, she had to chuckle.

"Isn't this a great day?" Matthew asked, casting his eyes upward toward the clear blue sky.

"Yes, it is. It's perfect," she answered, nodding her head in agreement.

Amy's attention focused on her husband. She gazed upon him

with adoration, and marveled at how handsome Matthew looked no matter what he was wearing or doing.

She thought his mischievous grin to be irresistibly devastating. His lips would curve upward at one corner of his mouth before breaking into a broad smile which would always cause Amy to catch her breath. She was elated that his dazzling smile had been appearing more frequent during the last few months.

Watching him now, she saw beads of moisture shining as gems across Matthew's bronzed back and broad shoulders, but she knew he didn't mind the toil and heat. It was undoubtedly a labor of love to him.

The large red barn bordered by the wooden rail corrals, along with lush green pastures nearby, were Matthew's prideful domain. He would count his herd of cattle each day with an enormous sense of pride and satisfaction.

Whenever a newborn calf was discovered, he would run to tell Amy the exciting news of the birth, and immediately she and Chrissie would have to rush to see the new arrival.

Upon the first calf's arrival, Matthew called Amy to the barnyard. "Come and look. We have another addition to our family...and fetch Chrissie. She's got to see the newborn, he said."

"Matt, I can't believe how cute he is. How can he walk when his legs are wobbling like that? Look, he can walk! Oh, he is absolutely adorable," Amy said amazingly.

This being the first time Chrissie had seen a real life calf, she was reluctant to come near until Amy urged her forward to better view the newborn calf.

Matthew beamed as he gestured to Chrissie to come closer. "Look, Chrissie, see the baby calf," he said.

"He looks just like the calf in your picture book," Amy said to Chrissie. "He is absolutely adorable, don't you agree?"

Chrissie squealed with delight. "Can I touch him, Mommy?"

"I'm sorry, Sweetie, not this time. He needs to get used to his surrounding first. I am sure he is frightened right now. Look at his wobbly legs. He is so cute."

"I like the baby calf, Daddy. Let's get more."

Amy never ceased to be enthralled over each new adventure that developed in their new life, the newborn calf incident being only one of several. She looked forward to each new day with an anticipation of delight.

Mischief showing upon his face, Matthew hoisted up the pitchfork, and called out with laughter in his voice to Amy, "Hey, I have a brilliant idea, Hon."

"And just what would that be?" Amy asked in a faked innocence, a suspicion entering her mind.

"Come help and I will teach you how to use this. This will just about fit your hand," he said teasingly, cupping the tool handle in his hand with a suggestive look on his face.

Giggling, Amy called back, shaking her head, "Oh no, not on your life. I have my own work cut out for me...right here."

Placing a protective hand to her belly, her face glowed radiantly as her lips curved into a wide, open smile. She was completely unaware of the captivating picture she made. She was absolutely beaming.

"Good excuse. I couldn't have thought of a better one myself," Matthew said teasingly.

"That's just about right. You had better get back to your own work, and I will learn from this distance, thank you very much."

"Chicken. Squawk, squawk," he said, mimicking like a hen flapping her wings. "You're afraid to try it out...afraid you might like it."

"Have fun all you want, but that pitchfork has your name written all over it. I wouldn't want to take that pleasure away from you," Amy countered back trying to pretend seriousness, but she was unable to refrain from bursting out laughing, knowing how much he delighted in teasing her. With a deep sigh of contentment, she leaned back against the porch column and watched Matthew for a while longer as he returned to his work.

Only a few weeks before, Amy had learned she was pregnant for the second time. When she surprised Matthew with the happy news, he couldn't have been more elated.

During the early stage of her pregnancy however, Amy

was having some minor difficulties. Her concerned obstetrician warned her that she would have to rest as much as possible to avoid a possible miscarriage. She was warned, also, to avoid any unnecessary stress or excitement for the sake of the baby, and for herself, as well.

Nevertheless, Amy felt quite confident that everything would be all right. After all, she couldn't have felt better.

Glancing now at her wristwatch, Amy saw that she would have enough time to heed her doctor's orders and take a short nap before she started preparing dinner. Reluctantly, she went back indoors.

Before going to her bedroom to lie down, she entered the nursery to check on Chrissie who was already napping. Leaning over the sleeping child, Amy thought how cherubic she looked in her peaceful sleep. Amy lovingly brushed away the damp golden locks that were pressed to Chrissie's rosy cheeks with her fingertips, and then she ran her fingertips gently over her tranquil face.

Amy saw clutched in the child's chubby arms the hideous rag doll with yellow yarn hair and crudely painted features on the face...the doll Amy found revolting...and Chrissie loved so much.

Lizzie Thornton had given this particular doll to Chrissie. Amy often wondered why the old recluse had given it to her. Perhaps, Amy speculated, it was because Chrissie may have reminded the elderly woman of the daughter she had lost. On the other hand, perhaps this same doll may have belonged to Lizzie's daughter before she had died.

It was evident that the doll wasn't new, for the body showed proof of repeated laundering. The doll's dress was yellowed with age, and a few stitches in the seams had been mended. The braided yarn hair was dull and frayed.

Amy and Matthew had seen the woman only a few times, mostly when she was walking the five miles to town, or when she was returning. She always refused their offers for a ride, always indicating she didn't want, nor need any favors from them.

"Are you sure you don't want a ride? We would be happy to give you a ride to wherever you need to go because we are going into town ourselves," Matthew said to her on more than one occasion.

"No. Thanks just the same, but I'd rather walk."

"All right, but it is a bit far to walk, and there's no need for you to have to walk when you can ride."

"I don't mind the walk. I'm used to it. I've been doing it for years," the old woman answered, walking on doggedly.

Not wanting to appear forceful, Amy and Matthew ceased their offers after several refusals, and they and Lizzie went on in their separate way.

The scrawny woman was in her sixties, but she looked much older than her years. Her body was frail and bent, her face, etched and weatherworn. Her hair had once been a shining raven black, but now was becoming a coarse and unruly gray with only a peppering of black remaining. She would look upon another with piercing dark eyes as if she was suspicious of anyone who would encounter her.

On one occasion, Matthew, with Chrissie accompanying him, drove up the lane to Lizzie Thornton's house to inquire about a missing calf. The aged woman half-heartedly invited them into her clean, but cluttered, kitchen so that she could continue her watch over a boiling kettle on the stove. She motioned toward one of the chairs set at the large oak table.

The table and chairs dominated the center of the room. Upon the table were filled bottles of tonic and a large basket of dried herbs that were really to be taken into the farmer's market in Spring Hill.

Matthew gazed curiously about the room. A cupboard next to the stove drew his attention. It was cluttered with various labeled, and a few unlabeled, jars and bottles of tonics, ointments, and poisons. A mortar and pestle lay in the midst of more bottles on a side table set against a wall.

He saw, suspended from the ceiling over the smaller table, several bunches of herbs that were hung to dry. Heaped under and alongside the table, were sacks of roots ready to add to the concoctions she would brew.

The scent of the drying herbs was strong in the air... rosemary, thyme, bay leaf and sage, along with a large assortment of wild herbs Lizzie gathered from the meadows, pastures, and roadways.

"Have a seat. I have to keep an eye on this, or it will boil over," Lizzie said as she returned to her task at the stove, occasionally swatting at a settling fly.

As Matthew pulled a chair out from the table and turned it about, he detected the spicy and sweet pungent odor of the herbs and roots, yet with a strong undercurrent of something bitter, yet sweet. He wasn't familiar with the scent, and coupled along with whatever was boiling on the stove, the stench was unpleasant to him.

Chrissie, shy in the presence of the old woman, immediately clambered upon Matthew's lap, and with her rounded blue eyes, stared at the strange woman. She, like her father, noticed the strong unfamiliar smells that were frightening to her.

"I won't take your time, Mrs. Thornton. The reason I'm here is that I'm missing a white-faced calf, and I wondered if it had gotten through the fence into your pasture," Matthew said as he sat down. "I thought you might have seen it around."

"Well, I could have...but no, I don't remember seeing it," Lizzie answered nonchalantly, continuing to stir the boiling concoction.

She turned her eyes away from the pot and glanced at the man and child sitting at the table. Almost as an afterthought, she turned her eyes to the small girl as if she had only now noticed her. The crease in her etched forehead deepened as she contemplatively studied the child.

She became lost in time, when there had existed another little girl who had looked much like this child who was clinging to her father. Her Elizabeth had been dark-haired, whereas this child was fair. While her penetrating eyes gazed upon Chrissie, the small child's features faded from Lizzie's vision, being replaced with her own beloved child's face.

Hurriedly, Lizzie forced her eyes away from the child to return to watch the boiling concoction. However, she couldn't refrain from glancing periodically at Chrissie. She pondered awhile before removing the long-handled wooden spoon from the boiling liquid and turned down the flame under the pot. She walked slowly over to where Matthew was seated with Chrissie on his lap.

Peering closely at the child, Lizzie said, "You sure are a pretty little girl. What is your name?"

"Chrissie," the child, shrinking away from the old woman's nearness, dutifully answered in a hesitant small voice. Even though Chrissie was within her father's protective arms, she recoiled against his chest.

A few moments later, Matthew, realizing he wasn't accomplishing anything with his inquiry about the missing animal, set Chrissie on her feet as he rose to leave. Chrissie clutched his hand tightly and tugged, urging him to hurry. She wanted to leave this smelly place as soon as possible.

"We must go now, Mrs. Thornton. Thank you for your time. I would appreciate you letting me know if you should happen to see the calf."

"Sure, I will, but I doubt if it will show up. Things have a way of disappearing around here...or dying. Once they're gone, they, more than likely, are gone for good," Lizzie answered, as she swept her veiled eyes back and forth as if she was expecting something or someone to appear.

Matthew thought her remark, in addition to her behavior, was somewhat bizarre. As with his small daughter, he was eager to return to the comfort of their own home, so he shrugged it off for the time being. Chrissie had clutched his hand tightly, and was urging him to hurry.

"Thanks for your time, Mrs. Thornton. I know you have a lot of work to do," Matthew said as he and Chrissie started for the door, reminding her again, "You will remember to let me know if you see the calf?"

Nodding, Lizzie fixed her eyes pointedly at the child, considering. She thought that Chrissie was such a sweet little girl and thought that her Elizabeth wouldn't mind...in fact, she felt confident that it would be what Elizabeth would have wanted her to do.

"Wait a minute, Mr. McCormack," Lizzie said after coming to a quick decision. "Don't leave yet. I have something...Wait here, I'll be right back."

Not waiting for a response, Lizzie turned and hurried from the room, leaving Matthew and Chrissie waiting hesitantly by the front door.

Waiting for her return, Matthew heard sounds of doors banging and drawers being pulled open from the next room from where Lizzie had disappeared. He was puzzled by her comment, *I have something*, and he wondered what she had in mind.

After a short while, Lizzie, with satisfaction written on her face, returned bearing a cloth doll with painted features upon it.

"Here, little one, this is for you. It has yellow hair just like yours," Lizzie said as she held the doll out to Chrissie. A slight quiver appeared on Lizzie's lips, as a momentary look of sadness and discomfort crossed her age-lined face.

Chrissie cautiously reached out to accept the doll from the smiling woman. The child she was, Chrissie was intrigued with the doll despite the ugliness and condition of it.

"What do you say, Chrissie?" Matthew asked, prompting the child to thank Lizzie for the gift. He was astounded with the kind and unexpected gesture from the old woman.

Beaming over the doll, Chrissie looked up at the woman. With a shy smile, she obediently said in a low voice, "Thank you for the dolly. I like it," before she tugged at Matthew's hand again and whispered loud enough for both to hear, "Daddy, can we go home now?"

"Oh, and for you and your wife...Here, take this. It is a tonic that I made myself. It will cure whatever ails you," Lizzie said, taking a brown bottle from her array of jars and bottles on the table and proudly handed it to Matthew.

Although he felt uncomfortable accepting the bottle of tonic, Matthew knew it would have been ill mannered of him to refuse the gift. He, therefore, politely accepted the tonic bottle, guessing that Amy would know what to do with it.

When Matthew and Chrissie returned home bearing their gifts, Amy took one whiff of the foul-smelling potion and turned up her nose. Shuddering, she jerked her head away.

"No one in this family is going to drink that stuff--especially from that woman. Who knows what is in that bottle," Amy said in determination.

Amy immediately carried the brown bottle outdoors and emptied the nauseating contents onto the ground, shuddering again at the sight and smell. Watching the thick green liquid slowly spreading on the ground, she noticed a strange iridescent coloring playing upon the slimy surface, appearing to eerily come alive.

Later that day, Matthew found their barnyard cat dead. They could only speculate if the sudden death of the cat had been related to the tonic. Amy had a strong suspicion that it had.

#

Bestowing a loving stroke to Chrissie's head, Amy stepped softly from the nursery. She continued to her own bedroom and stretched out on top of the soft downy comforter, her head sinking luxuriously into the softness of the pillow.

Waiting for sleep to claim her, Amy's mind drifted with serene and happy thoughts as she became groggy. When she finally succumbed to sleep, her last thoughts were of how happy they all were…and that their lives were going extremely well. It couldn't have been more perfect.

It was almost too perfect….

Chapter 3

Matthew McCormack was no stranger to the farm life. He had been born and reared in Kansas, and his plans had been to buy his own land in Kansas after graduating from college. He did various part-time jobs, such as harvesting, as well as hauling hay and cattle, in order to reach that goal.

Those plans, however, were shattered when his family's home was destroyed by a tornado that left his parents destitute. Feeling it was his obligation to do what he could, he helped them to relocate upstate. The insurance that they received not being nearly enough to suffice, he good-heartedly gave his parents his long-saved money to replace all the belongings they had lost. Left short on funds because of his good deed, he had to delay purchasing his own farm estate a while longer.

Deciding that he would have to make it big if he was ever going to be able to buy his own place, he headed to the big city. New York City. Determined to be a successful and wealthy businessman, he confidently put his former life behind him for the time being.

During the next few years, Matthew worked diligently to become a success in hope that in time, he would be able to return to Kansas and purchase his own farm.

Then he found Amy. With her in his life, he put aside his dreams of returning to Kansas to make a life with her. After all, he decided a life with Amy was far more important than farming in a rural environment.

Amy was the only child of a wealthy senator and his wife, a well-known judicial judge. As a result, she led a very sheltered life until the fateful day she received word that her parent's private jet had crashed en route to Lake Tahoe for a much needed vacation. Both were killed instantly, leaving Amy alone without any immediate family for whom she could depend upon.

Upon their deaths, Amy was suddenly faced with having to learn to fend for herself. Determinately, she grimly set about building a new life for herself. Being a determined and courageous young woman, she decided she could, and would, succeed. After all, whom else, but herself, could she turn to?

Then, she met Matthew McCormack. It was love at first sight for both of them, and they were married shortly thereafter. They couldn't have been more right for each other; they were destined to be together. Their lives became more perfect after their beautiful baby daughter came into the world…until gradually, little by little, the dreams he had put behind him began to resurface.

Much as he tried, Matthew could never erase the sounds, smells, and tastes of the farm life from his mind. He had never realized until now how much he would miss the farm, and how much it had been a part of his life and his happiness.

Whether at the breakfast table, or in front of the fireplace, Matthew reflected endlessly, telling Amy about his experiences of living on the farm in Kansas.

Captivated by the many stories he told, she knew it had to be a different way of life from what she was used to. Growing up in a prominent home in New York City, she had never been interested in the rural life; therefore, she had been away from her city domain only a few times.

"Do people really live like that?" Amy would ask in disbelief as Matthew would tell stories, often exaggerating somewhat, about the past life he had known and loved.

"Yes, Amy, they do. No hustle and bustle, just the simple life. There, you just live each day as it comes. Everything is so peaceful there in the country. It's not at all like it is here," he explained.

It amazed her how anyone could live like that. There were too many inconveniences. She could not imagine having to do their own laundry instead of having laundry service. It was unspeakable to not have a cleaning service, nor having a nanny for Chrissie.

"How could you have loved living in a place where there are only outdoor privies?" Amy asked, remembering all the stories Matthew had told her. "That is disgusting."

Matthew only grinned at her vivid imagination, as she, once

started, couldn't stop talking about what she pictured farm life in Kansas to be. Listening to her, one would think she was speaking about an entirely different country.

"I suppose horses and cows wouldn't be that bad. But, Matthew, I can't imagine having nasty chickens practically in one's backyard. Ugh." She couldn't help but shudder.

"Honey, it isn't that bad. Besides, you would get used to it," Matthew said, breaking into a peal of laughter."

"I really don't think it's that funny. Thank goodness, we don't have to live that way. How can you even think that would be peaceful?"

"Oh, but it is peaceful and quiet. The closest neighbors would be a mile away, or a half-mile, at the least. Sometimes, you might not even see a soul for a week."

Amy face contorted with disbelief, not knowing whether to believe what he was telling her, or if he was teasing her.

"I can just picture you in blue jeans and your hair in pigtails, milking a cow, or you in the pigpen with all that muddy muck oozing between your pretty toes, feeding slop to the hogs," Matthew said, teasing her without mercy.

Watching Amy in her daily ritual of coiling her blond hair into an elegant chignon and securing the coiffure with pins, he doubled over with laughter thinking how hysterically funny it would be to see her living on a real farm and handling the daily chores.

"Don't even think it," Amy glared back at Matthew through the dressing table mirror. "That is absolutely disgusting. You will never see me anywhere near any of that. Oh, how revolting!" The images she got from it caused her to cringe.

Matthew, howling with uncontrollable laughter, continued to provoke Amy until she realized he was teasing. Blushing, she shyly returned to finishing her toiletries.

"Well, it would be an interesting sight. Who knows, you just might like it…and stop shooting daggers at me with those sexy blue eyes."

Chuckling, Matthew, with a devilish look, returned her gaze

before his face clouded with yearning. Without expressing his thoughts aloud, he wished it could be.

Realizing that he missed that former life tremendously, he knew that it would never be possible for him to go back to that way of life. He had to consider his wife and daughter, and what they were achieving in their careers. Their lives were in New York City, and that was where they would have to stay. Before she would notice his change of mood, he quickly tried to disguise his wistfulness with a thin smile.

"I think you had better quit playing around and be off to work, my dear husband," she said, turning toward him. The amusement died from her eyes when she detected his look of sadness, and she was puzzled by his abrupt change of mood. She regarded him with searching gravity, as a sudden tension overtook the room.

Knowing what the consequences would be if she pursued it, she chose to remain silent, and tried to put it out of her mind. His constant mysterious musings were becoming annoying to her, as they were occurring more frequently.

With a strained silence, she rose from her vanity, and selected a tailored suit from her closet. Hurriedly, she began dressing, as not to be late for work herself, while at the same time, confusing thoughts whirled in her mind.

Time after time, she had asked him what was wrong. He would only close up on her, refusing to tell her anything. Often, she would put the blame on herself, wondering if it was she, if she had disappointed him in some way.

Both Matthew and Amy were successful in the business world because of their hard work and dedication. Matthew owned a promising architectural engineering firm, besides being actively involved with the stock market. With his busy time schedule, it left little time for his family.

Loving her career as an interior designer for a major company, Amy dreamed of someday owning her own company, and making a big name for herself. She worked diligently to become the best in her field. But her career did not stop her from being a devoted wife and mother, always putting her family first and foremost.

With their careers and their lives continuing the way it was, Amy and Matthew should have been happy and content, but unfortunately, something was missing. What had started out as a happy and loving marriage was now in serious trouble. They didn't see one another enough, and when they did, communication between them was almost nonexistent. Their lack of communication created a stressful relationship that continued to worsen.

At work, Matthew would push himself beyond exhaustion, but whatever the reason was, Amy could not imagine, other than sensing his dissatisfaction and unhappiness. Clueless as to why, she worried about him. Being concerned for him, she had repeatedly asked him to confide in her, but he always refrained from talking about what was troubling him.

"I'm just tired. It's been a long day," he would say, after coming home night after night, exhausted and irritable.

"Matthew, why can't you come home earlier? Is it necessary to stay overtime like you have been doing? You're pushing yourself much too hard."

"For God's sake, how many times do I have to tell you? I have too much to do. I can't just get up and walk out as you would want, or think I can."

"But, you don't have to push yourself the way you are. We have all that we need...this beautiful penthouse...and more importantly, we have Chrissie. Please be a father to her. Don't neglect her because of your work. We hardly see you anymore."

"I don't want to go through this again. I said I'm tired. Okay?"

Amy could see the strain of overwork in Matthew's eyes. Fatigue settled in deep pockets under his eyes. The eyes that used to be full of sparkle were now dulling. Deep furrowing lines on his forehead were becoming more apparent each day, and he seldom smiled.

"Matthew, what is wrong? Why aren't you happy? Please talk to me about it. We can work this out together. Just give me a chance to help you."

"Nothing is wrong. I said I was tired. Just drop it, will you? I just can't help it. There is never enough time to get all my work finished. There are such things as deadlines to meet."

"But, you don't have to kill yourself in the process. You're always tired and overworked. Please, Matthew, slow down. You do have people working for you. Can't you delegate some of the workload to them?"

"I would like to, but how? This is my work, so that makes it my responsibility. It has to be done. You know as well as I do that if I don't do it myself, the work just won't be done. I have no other choice. Please try to understand, Amy."

"I do understand, but I don't want us to get to the point of losing everything that is important to us. I mean our marriage-- our life together. This is not doing either of us any good," Amy answered.

By not communicating with Amy as he should have, he didn't realize what it was doing to her, or to him. He diligently refused to admit or talk about his unhappiness; therefore, leaving her in the dark. His increasing state of denial was leading him into a deep depression. He felt that she would never understand if he did try to explain. And besides, what could she do even if she could understand?

The late nights continued to occur, and their marriage became more strained. Amy's heart ached for Matthew as she worried about him. She had no idea as to why he felt he had to push himself at such a pace, other than realizing that he wanted, and needed, to succeed, but after awhile she saw that he couldn't continue this way, nor could she.

One night, Amy asked, "Where were you, Matthew? It is very late, and your dinner is cold, as usual. I tried to keep it warm and now--"

"Oh, stop it, Amy. Will you just quit badgering me? I had to work late, so just leave me alone," Matthew barked, his temper flaring.

"You're drunk! You reek with liquor. You've been lying to me, haven't you? All this time I thought you were working. I can't believe you would do that to me," Amy said, shocked and angry. "How could you?"

Glaring at him with hostility, her anger became a scalding fury. She was thoroughly disgusted with his drunkenness and appearance. She wondered if this was what she would have to face in the future.

"Oh, quit your whining. I am sick and tired of it. You don't know what you are talking about. If you want to know, I am tired of hearing your bitching. You are always complaining about something. Just leave it."

"Matthew!" Her mouth flew open in disbelief when she heard his rude accusations. "How can you say that? I'm only thinking about you. I'm concerned about what is happening to you...and to us."

"Well, don't be. You are always nagging. Just stop it."

Overwrought with anger and hurt, she could only stand there in the middle of the living room, stunned and unable to speak further. She couldn't believe that he was actually making these foul accusations, for he had never spoken in that way before.

"I'm sorry, Amy. I shouldn't have said that. Let's just forget it."

She was unable to respond. Too much had been said, and she couldn't accept what it was doing to them. And she definitely couldn't forget it.

Suddenly, Matthew reached out and roughly grasped her arm, sneering, "Don't I even get a sweet little kiss from you tonight? Come here, Baby, give me some sugar, or better yet..."

He looked at Amy with a sardonic expression that, along with his drunkenness, sent her temper soaring more. Struggling free from his grasp, her blue eyes blazing, she faced him furiously.

"Don't you dare touch me, you drunken fool. You are despicable this way and I can't take any more of what you are doing to me. I've spent months worrying about you, and you can't care less," Amy said as she spat out the words contemptuously, while tears of fury and humiliation blinded her eyes.

Sobbing uncontrollably, she turned abruptly and fled from the room to the confinement of their bedroom, slamming the door behind her.

Upon hearing the door slam, it immediately sobered him. Realizing what he had done, he was remorseful, and he started to call her back to apologize.

"Amy, I'm--" His words died when he heard her lock the door between them. He couldn't go on. Standing motionless, he could merely murmur, "Never mind, she would never understand."

Alone in their bedroom, Amy threw herself onto the bed and yielded to the compulsive sobs that shook her. She was in anguish wondering where this constant arguing was going to leave them. Will it always be like this, or will it only get worse? Without a doubt, she had to find out what was troubling him and destroying their marriage. Whatever it was, she saw that it was tormenting him deeply. Amy had become more aware with each day that their marriage was deteriorating before her eyes, and if it was to be saved, something would have to be done, and soon. But, what could she do? Was it already too late?

Falling asleep after restless hours of tossing and turning worrying about Matthew, she began to dream, a muddled, meaningless dream. Her body tensed as a dark, ominous cloud approached her and weighted down onto her chest, holding her prisoner, making it difficult for her to breathe.

After awakening the next morning, she was thoroughly confused about the dream she had. She reasoned it was because of her stress and worries. Having more important things to think about, she knew she should put the dream out of her mind. But, before she could, she had to question what the dream meant.

It was much like a warning of some kind. But, could it have been? No, it was too ridiculous to even think that, she told herself. It was only a dream, and she shrugged it off as to have been because of her anxiety.

Chapter 4

Pushing herself relentlessly to take her mind off her problems, Amy, much like Matthew, would come home many evenings completely exhausted. But, no matter how busy she was, she always took time to spend time with Chrissie. Amy had sworn to herself she was not going to neglect her daughter as Matthew often did.

It became a ritual that every night she would have to prepare dinner and wait to see if Matthew was going to come home before his dinner became cold. Their lives had become a very dull, stressful, and predictable routine. They seldom went out together, and whenever they did, there would always be very little conversation between them. The sparkle of them enjoying time with each other was no longer there.

Matthew's hours at the office grew longer and longer, or he was out getting drunk, not wanting to go home. Night after night, his dinner would congeal as it got cold. Without doubt, Amy and Matthew's marriage was doomed.

#

One autumn evening, after finishing another warmed-over meal and putting Chrissie to bed, Amy and Matthew sat musing in silence before the crackling fire in the fireplace, each lost in his and her thoughts.

Amy was absentmindedly turning the pages of <u>House Beautiful</u>, not focusing on anything on the pages, while Matthew, with a far-away look in his eyes was staring into the orange flames flickering on the fire logs.   There was a painful quiet in the room. The only sound came from the rustle of the magazine pages and the crackle and sizzle of the glowing flames in the fireplace.

"The trees back home are most likely turning color now," Matthew said in a voice that seemed to come from a long way off. He was unaware that he had spoken aloud.

A suggestion of annoyance hovering in her eyes, Amy looked up from the magazine pages and turned her attention to him. Her immediate thought was of his dreaming of The Farm--again.

That was all he could talk about, or cared about anymore. Even more than his family. Quickly chastising herself for her annoyance upon seeing the wistfulness on his somber face, she refrained from saying anything. It would only upset them both.

A look of tired sadness passing over his face, Matthew turned to face Amy. His eyes upon her, he paused a moment to reflect before he turned back to gaze at the fireplace. Watching the warm hues of the flickering flames, he could see images of the colorful autumn leaves swirling among the flames.

"You can't imagine how beautiful the trees are this time of the year. The red maples, the gold and orange leaves of the oaks...You just can't imagine," Matthew said softly, his face growing tranquil, as he visualized the scene of which he was familiar. "I wish you could see it."

"Where?" Amy asked as she closed the magazine and dropped it in her lap.

"The countryside. It doesn't matter. Forget it."

Amy gazed at Matthew sitting in front of the fireplace, with a faraway look in his eyes. Seeing the silent sadness written on his face, and on his hunched body, she felt empathy for him. Trying to visualize what Matthew was seeing, she shifted her gaze to the bright orange flames flickering on the crackling logs. She wondered if it was possible that the answer to what was making him unhappy lay in Kansas, where he had lived most of his life. She grew thoughtful for a few minutes before she spoke. She had an idea.

"Maybe we could..."

"Could what?" Matthew asked as he came out of his reveries and turned toward Amy. Without much enthusiasm, he waited for her to finish what she was about to say.

"Let's go on a vacation. We could go somewhere...maybe to the country?" she suggested, thinking maybe this is just what he needs. A vacation to visit his home place just might be the answer to what she was looking for. She hadn't realized until now that maybe he missed his home after all these years. She hesitated a moment before continuing. She had to continue before she lost her courage. "Maybe we could go to...Kansas?"

She was stunned that she actually made the suggestion, but Matthew was beyond that. He was flabbergasted.

In complete astonishment, he stared at Amy. He was not sure if he had heard her correctly. Upon searching her pale face, however, he saw seriousness displayed upon it, followed by hesitancy before ending with courageousness.

"What did you say? Did you say what I thought you did? Would you really want to go to Kansas? You never wanted to go before, so why now?" Matthew asked, astounded when he realized she was indeed serious. His eyes slowly lighting up like the flames in the fireplace, he eagerly searched her face in utter disbelief.

A smile finding its way through her mask of uncertainty, Amy nodded her head affirmatively, and answered, "Yes, Matt. Maybe you could show me a real live farm. Don't you think it is time I saw one after all you have told me about Kansas? Besides, I want to see if what you had told me about Kansas is true."

It took Matthew a moment to grasp what Amy was saying and whether what he was hearing was real.

"This is too unbelievable. I never thought you would even consider going there," Matthew, said in amazement.

Unable to contain his excitement, leaped to his feet, and began to pace around the room. He pulled Amy from the chair where she had been sitting and enclosed her into the circle of his arms, embracing her tightly and showering kisses over her face. First, he kissed her cheeks, then her eyes, and finally, he satisfyingly kissed her soft mouth.

"Amy, I love you."

Amy happily relished the moment because he hadn't treated her with that much enthusiasm for a long while. Her heart fluttering wildly in her breast, she pulled away laughingly, knowing they had much to decide and to plan. Elated, she knew then that she had made the right decision.

"Hey, let me go, Matt. It's only a vacation."

"Amy, you don't know how much this means to me. You'll love it, I promise you will."

Plans of places they would go and things they would see were already formulating in his mind.

"We will have to make arrangements at our offices. When do you think we will be able to leave, Matt? There shouldn't be any problems in getting away, should there?"

"No, Honey, I am positive there wouldn't be anything to prevent us from going," Matthew answered, his face beaming with excitement.

"I don't think it would be a problem for me to be gone, either. I think it would be ideal if we could leave as soon as we can if that is all right with you." Before I change my mind, she thought.

"That would be great. How about leaving this weekend? Oh, this is fantastic. Do you think we can be ready by then?"

Amy answered, "I don't see why we couldn't." She was just anxious to go and get this over with, not caring whether she was going to enjoy this so-called vacation. She just wanted him to be happy.

"I can't believe we are at last going to Kansas, Amy. We can make a short stop at my parents while we are there. Why hadn't we done this before? Chrissie will--"

"Wait," Amy said, interrupting him, "Let's not take Chrissie with us this time. I would like to...Matt, we need the time to ourselves. Would it be all right with you that we don't take her with us this time?"

Contemplating about what she was suggesting, Matthew's mood grew solemn as he responded, "Yes, I agree that we do. I think it is a wonderful idea that we leave her here. It will be like a second honeymoon." Matthew said, as he smiled suggestively. Giving her a conspiratorial wink, he added, "Say, purdy gal, reckon we kin find us a hay loft in some old barn somewhere to do some...uh...relaxin'?"

"All right, wise guy, quit your pathetic attempt at mimicking, and get serious," Amy answered in sternly pretense, going along with his game, but unable to continue the charade, she burst out laughing.

She felt a warm glow surge pass through her when she saw

Matthew's intense pleasure, and she gloried briefly in the shared moment. Her eyes meeting his, she felt a ray of hope within her for the first time that this could possibly be the way to save their rocky marriage. It was only a vacation. What did she have to lose?

Matthew's remark about the second honeymoon echoed through her mind. The implications of it sent waves of excitement through her, but she had to control her emotions for the moment. There would be time for such thoughts later. For now, they had other things they needed to do.

"I'll call Chrissie's nanny first thing in the morning, Matt. I know she won't mind staying with the little squirt and, need I mention, spoiling her more."

"Thank you for suggesting this and I promise you won't be sorry. I love you, my wonderful Amy," Matthew said with deep conviction in his voice. He felt that he could not express his gratitude enough to her.

Once again, she found herself in his strong arms. As they embraced, a slender delicate thread of hope began to form within her. Caught up in his enthusiasm, Amy knew she was doing the right thing, but questions intervened.

Will it be enough to save their marriage? After the vacation ends, then what? Where will they go from there?

Chapter 5

"Oh, Matt, you were right. It is incredible," Amy exclaimed, her blue eyes shimmering with awareness, as her gaze swept from one side of the road to the other.

As they drove through the majestic countryside, Amy was enthralled with the breathtaking beauty of the trees, their autumn leaves brilliantly displayed against the dazzling blue sky. She was spellbound seeing cattle and horses grazing in the open expanse of green meadows, giving her a sense of tranquility and freedom.

With the top down on their convertible, the wind lifted her blond hair, tossing it around in disarray, and into her face. She did not care because she felt uninhabited and exhilarated.

She glanced at Matthew to find him watching her glowing face that revealed an enjoyment of his own. Amy saw a sparkle in his eyes, something she hadn't seen in a long, long while--and his smile--She hadn't seen that smile as brilliant and tantalizing as it was now. At that moment, she couldn't resist the temptation to reach over to kiss him quickly on the cheek.

"Nice...but, what was that for?"

"It's because you brought me here, and I'm happy because you are happy. Besides that, your smile is irresistible."

"I love you, Amy, and I love you even more for suggesting this fantastic vacation. I'm happy that you are enjoying it."

"I love you too, Matt, and I can't agree more. It's been awesome. I could never have imagined anything more splendid. It is like...a painting. Wouldn't it be great to have a painting just like this to hang in our living room?" Amy said, gesturing at their surroundings.

She swept her gaze from side to side, trying to savor each wonderful moment as they traveled through the spacious countryside of southern Kansas.

"I'd get it for you if I could, but I think I could manage the real thing. How would you like that?" he teased, hiding his inner misery.

"Hey there, you can try all you want, but it's just not going to work. You thought you could trick me, but I'm smarter than you realize," Amy said, smirking. "After all you have told me about living here on a farm? No...not on your life."

Amy, relaxing back in her seat, smiled as she thought about his remark. She thought how totally absurd it would be to live way out here in the middle of nowhere. For a vacation, it is wonderful, and she was enjoying every minute of it. But, to live here? Oh, no. She was convinced that he could tease all he wants, but that's as far as it will go.

Traveling through the countryside with which he was familiar, Matthew pointed out to Amy all the places he remembered from his earlier years. As they traveled through the rural towns, some large, some small, she was amazed. Some towns, being relatively small, consisted only of a post office, service station and convenience store--if even that.

The couple stopped at places along the way to purchase souvenirs for themselves, as well as for Chrissie. It would be unspeakable to return home without gifts for Chrissie.

They stopped at roadside parks and absorbed the beauty of the colorful display of autumn colors. They took numerous photographs of the landscapes, and of the various interesting landmarks. This fantastic vacation was one that they would never forget.

Amy loved the old-fashioned rustic motels and cafes that were quite different from her New York City skyscrapers and huge department stores. She was enthralled with it all.

As they passed farms with "For Sale" signs in front,
Matthew gazed with longing at what he wished could be his. Amy saw the desire written on his face, and she realized then that he had indeed come home.

A small part of her drawn up into his dream, she thought of the possibility of...

She shook herself. She had to stop thinking this way. It is too absurd. No, it simply would not work. She knew nothing about this way of life, and furthermore, they both had their careers to think about. It saddened dawned on her that they hadn't even missed their home and their careers, except for their daughter they had left behind with her nanny. Thinking that Chrissie would have enjoyed it as much as she did, Amy now wished they had brought her with them.

The next morning began as a glorious crisp autumn day. As she stepped outdoors, the brisk breeze caused Amy to catch her breath. She had never before felt the invigorating sensation with which she was experiencing at that moment.

As she inhaled the clean unpolluted air, Amy felt the tingle of the cool breeze upon her flesh. She felt renewed, and it felt marvelous. It was such a contrast to their home in New York City, where the smog-ridden air would cause her difficulty in breathing. The stark gray streets with everything concrete, where trees cannot grow, and the towering skyscrapers that prevented you from seeing, or feeling, the sunshine, made a strong contrast to what she was witnessing now.

"How can I go back to that?" she asked herself sadly. "Yet, we must go back--It is our home."

Continuing their tour through the countryside, Matthew and Amy passed picturesque farm estates, flat expanses of plowed fields, and many newly-sown fields of wheat. They passed by meadows with green grasses, not yet brown with dormancy, bending and swaying in the gentle wind. Gently rolling hills were blanketed with trees in all its splendor showing the breath-taking aura of autumn gilded with hues of reds, oranges, and russets. Green cedar trees dotted the terrain, complementing the bright autumn tones. All the hues of the rainbow were evident in the panoramic view, as they intertwined with the predominate colors of the autumn day.

Viewing the awesome beauty of nature, they continued snapping photographs, including photographs of each other depicting their happiness in the autumn settings.

If only that happiness could last forever, Amy thought wistfully, already thinking of when they would have to return home, and what would take place once they were back home. She was saddened to think of having to leave this splendor behind them, and that the time for their departure was drawing nearer much too quickly.

Chapter 6

The day came when the couple was to begin their journey homeward. They sadly loaded their belongings into the car, glancing about them with reluctance. They had to return to New York City, to their daughter, and to their jobs.

"Seeing all this uniqueness around us, I hate to leave," Amy said with a faint tremor in her voice. Casting her eyes about their surroundings, and taking in one last sweep of the colorful landscape, she felt she was leaving a part of herself. She couldn't explain the feeling that life would never be the same for her again.

"I know. I feel the same way," Matthew answered, his voice echoing her longing.

"I have never dreamed of anything more serene. I love it here, Matthew. It isn't at all like I had imagined."

"I knew you would like it. Didn't I tell you so?" Matthew answered, pleased that she did. A thin smile played upon Matthew's lips as he held the car door open for her to slide into the car. Shutting the door after her, he hesitated as he cast a final look around him, much as Amy had, before he entered the vehicle. It was time to go back home where they belonged, and to their jobs that were waiting.

"Honey, let's not go yet. Can we have a little more time before leaving? I don't want to leave yet. There is more to see, and I want to see it all."

Not eager to leave either, he answered, "I suppose a while longer won't hurt, but we will have to leave soon."

"Thank you, Matt. You were right, I do love it here. I could almost be willing to stay here...just almost."

A short while later while driving down graveled country road lined with pastures with grazing cattle and autumn-hued trees, Amy suddenly shouted, pointing to her right.

"Stop, Matt. Look at that."

Alarmed at her exclamation, Matthew slammed his foot hard on the brakes. Upon seeing what she was excited about, he was stunned by her outburst.

"Matthew, isn't it the most beautiful place you have ever seen?" she asked in awe.

Matthew maneuvered the vehicle over to the side of the road and stopped. The vehicle had barely come to a stop when Amy immediately leaped out and rushed a short distance from the car before she stopped to wait for Matthew to catch up with her.

In silence, they both stood in an enraptured wonder, as they gazed at what seemed much like a scene from a portrait, breathtaking in its panoramic splendor, a captivating farm estate surrounded by spacious meadows and bountiful awesome trees. Amy was mesmerized for she had never before seen such a spectacular sight as what lay before her.

Their gazes followed the long narrow lane that wound its way up the gentle incline, stopping in front of a charming two-story country manor. A wooden veranda wrapped around two sides of the white house. Supporting the veranda, there were two massive white columns flanking the front entrance to the house and the corners of the porch.

There was a magnificent maple tree ablaze with color in one corner of the rail-fenced yard. The spellbound couple turned their attention next to the large red hay barn situated at one end of the barnyard corral that was enclosed by wooden railings. They noticed other outbuildings...a towering silo, storage barns, a large garage that possibly housed vehicles, tractors and other farm equipment...whatever a farmer's heart would desire.

Matthew and Amy admired the magnificent trees bordering the land. Beautiful trees, majestic, yet tranquil-looking. Beyond the tree line they could distinguish a brown cornfield and, alongside it, they could see the large gently rolling expanse of a green meadow that looked as if it went on forever. In his mind's eye, Matthew could see cattle and horses grazing there--his.

It was everything Matthew had ever dreamed of. His mind wandered as he stared before him unseeing, the view before him becoming obscured by his fervent thoughts. For this, he wouldn't look twice at his job, and the money he was making. He would gladly trade it all for this. To hell with the city, and the same old day-to-day grind.

Matthew thought about the executive offices and the ringing telephones, and who in their right mind would choose the cold and hard grayness of concrete--and the stench of pollution--over this. He wondered what had been the matter with him for thinking he could live like that. He had been such a damn fool, but now it was too late to go back to what he had loved.

Unknown to him, Amy, also, was having similar thoughts of her own. She was, however, one step farther.

Could she do it? Would it be possible? Was she courageous enough to dare suggest it? Glancing over at her husband and seeing the yearning on his face, she knew what her answer would have to be. It undoubtedly would be a "yes".

"Matt, Darling. I've been thinking..." Amy said. "Do you suppose we could..."

Matthew turned toward Amy, his thoughts interrupted by her words. "Could what?"

"Well...this place is for sale. Look, there is a real estate sign. Could we take a closer look at the place...maybe?" There was an almost imperceptible note of pleading in her voice and on her face.

Surprised at her request, Matthew searched Amy's face in incredulity as to what she meant, and he saw that she was serious indeed. Anticipation crept into his thoughts. Amy, my city-breed Amy? No, that's absurd. She couldn't have meant it. He thought he must have misunderstood.

"Sure, Honey, if that's what you want. But, why?"

"You like it, don't you? I know I...I do. Let's go to that real estate office. The address is there on the sign. Please, let's look at it."

Amy's lip quivered as she shyly admitted to herself that she liked the place, even if it was in Kansas, and not in New York. She surprised herself that she had asked the favor to look more closely at the farm estate lying before them and to even consider what she had in mind.

"Amy, what are you saying? Would you actually be willing for us to perhaps buy this farm? To leave the city and our jobs behind...to move here? This is far from being like our penthouse, you do realize that?" Matthew asked, giving her a sidelong glance of utter disbelief. It was overwhelming to him in hearing her say she wanted to purchase the farm estate. This was what he had always dreamed about and desired, but now to have that possibly happen was absolutely incredible.

A smile trembling over her lips, Amy gave a tense nod of consent. She was frightened, yet she knew in her heart it was the right thing to do. There was no doubt in her mind that Matthew would be happy living here, and Chrissie would love it. Amy believed wholeheartedly that with time she could grow accustomed to this new life. As long as her husband was happy, she would be happy. More importantly, she felt that this may very well be the answer to saving their marriage.

"Do you think we would be able to afford it?" Amy questioned, growing more serious with each moment. "There is my inheritance we could use if we need."

"No, Amy, I'm sure that won't be necessary. We have our nest egg and with the investment dividends coming in...No, I don't think there would be a problem in making a down payment. I, more than likely, should have enough funds left over to buy what machinery I would need to get started, plus some cattle. If not, I could always get a loan," Matthew answered, already speculating of owning the estate that lay before them. He was visualizing his dream coming true.

"Could we go to the real estate office now? We do have time, don't we, Matt?" Being impatient, she needed to know right away whether this was, without a doubt, going to be their new home.

"All right, Baby, let's go see this real estate man and find out what he has to say."

Matthew gave Amy a quick hug as they hurried to the car. He still could not believe that this was actually happening. Smiling mischievously, he couldn't resist adding, "Just maybe I'll make a country gal out of you yet."

On the way to the realtor's office in Spring Hill, Amy nervously tidied her windblown hair by arranging it into a neat chignon. It was when she was retouching her lipstick that a thought entered her mind.

Amy closed the cover of her make-up compact with a snap and slowly replaced it into her bag. A serious expression appearing upon her face, she looked up at Matthew, and spoke in a weak and tremulous whisper.

"Matthew, there is just one thing…"

"Yes, Hon, what's that?"

"I've got to have indoor plumbing…please."

Chapter 7

"I'll be with you in jus' a minute," the elderly realtor, covering the mouthpiece of the telephone, said as he greeted the McCormacks.

Returning to the phone conversation he had been engaged in when Amy and Matthew entered his office, Harry Deakins observed the couple and knew instantly that they weren't local people. They looked much different from the local people of Spring Hill.

The handsome young man had a look of eminence about him…the way he dressed, the way he held his head, his mannerisms. The elegant young woman was exquisite as she carried a regal certainty…her pale oval face revealing both delicacy and strength. Unconsciously gazing at her, the elderly realtor passed his free hand nervously over his thinning gray hair. He had almost forgotten he was holding the telephone receiver in his hand, nor did it occur to him to offer seats to the couple.

He couldn't tear his gaze away from the woman standing before him…from her elegantly upswept blond hair which accentuated her arresting face to her expensive-looking off-white pantsuit that emphasized her slender body. Seeing people like them in his small hometown was rare. Scrutinizing the couple, he thought there could be no mistake about them. This couple spelled class.

Hurriedly freeing himself from the telephone conversation, Harry Deakins exchanged handshakes with Matthew and Amy. Pulling out chairs for them, he, then, seated himself behind the cluttered desk that was piled high with papers and folders. Feeling embarrassed that the stylish couple saw the messiness of his desk, he shifted his papers nervously. Surveying the couple, he thought that surely they were here for reasons other than for real estate. He wondered why classy people like them would want real estate in rural Kansas, but concluded that there were all kinds of people in this world.

Remembering Matthew's jesting the night before they left New York City, Amy had to smile to herself upon hearing the elderly man's dialect. Glancing toward Matthew, she wondered whether it, also, had crossed his mind, but she could tell by the eager expression on his face that his thoughts were only on the farm estate they had seen.

"What can I do for you today? You in the market for some real estate property?" he asked, anxiously waiting for their reply.

"My wife and I have been driving around the area and saw a place...a farm you have listed for sale. You have a 'For Sale' sign in front. From what we saw from the road, we're impressed with the farm, and we wondered if we may possibly have a closer look at it today."

"Why, of course I'll be glad to show you whatever I've got. What place is it that you wanna see?"

"It's the farm with the large white two-story house with a veranda. It sits off from the road. There is a magnificent red maple tree in the front yard," Amy answered in a rushed tone. "There is a white fence and barn, and we--"

"There is a large hay meadow and a wheat field," Matthew said, interrupting Amy, as he excitedly grasped her hand, giving it a quick gentle squeeze.

"Oh, yeah, that one. I know the place you're talkin' 'bout," Harry answered, his gray eyebrows pulling into a frown.

Her breath catching in her throat, panic mounted inside Amy when she caught the realtor's expression. Two lines of worry appeared between her eyes. Leaning forward, she asked, "It is still for sale, isn't it, Mr. Deakins?"

"Gee, folks, I'm real sorry, but that property's already been sold. Got a contract with a down payment on it jus' yesterday. I jus' haven't gotten out there yet to put up the 'Sold' sign," he said, apologetically. "Gee, I'm real sorry."

He regretted having to give this kind of news to the young couple sitting on the other side of the desk. He clearly saw the disappointment written on their faces and sympathized for them. It was clear in his mind that they had fallen in love with that old place, for whatever reason, he couldn't understand.

Tears welling in Amy's downcast eyes, she groped for Matthew's trembling hand. Neither was able to speak. They had found their dream...and lost it...all within the same day. They were both devastated.

The kind realtor sensing their heartbreak wished he could somehow ease their disappointment. He thought that maybe he could convince them to consider other farms, if a farm was what they wanted, and he started searching among the papers on his desk.

"I've got other places for sale. Maybe you'd like to look at some of 'em? Here is one I think you--"

"No, thank you," Matthew answered grimly, "We wouldn't be interested in any other, at least for now. Maybe we will at some later date."

If ever.

Clasping his hands and staring unseeingly at them, Matthew felt drained, hollow, and lifeless, unable to think of anything except the farm they would not have. He had come so close to having what he had always desired, and now it was gone.

"Thank you, Mr. Deakins," Amy said, her voice starting to break. "This is...was the one we wanted." She quickly rose from her seat. Unable to say more, she abruptly turned away and rushed out the door before either man could see the tears flowing down her cheeks.

A lump forming in his throat, Matthew, also, was eager to make his exit before he betrayed his emotions to the stranger. After a few strained cordial words with the realtor, Matthew rose to leave. After exchanging business cards, Matthew gave his thanks and hurried out the door after his wife.

Amy stood leaning back against the hood of their car in despair and tried to brush away her tears. When Matthew saw her anguish, he took her into his arms to give, as well as to receive, comfort. His embrace was almost unbearable in its tenderness. Amy buried her face into Matthew's chest and wept her heart out. She couldn't tell him how much this farm meant to her. She didn't know, herself, until just a few moments ago.

Not only did she fall in love with the old farmhouse, but more importantly, it was to have been a new beginning for her and Matthew--and a chance to save their faltering marriage.

"I'm sorry, Honey," Matthew said consolingly against her hair. "Maybe it just wasn't meant to be. Eventually we may find something else...something we will like even better."

"No, I'm sorry, Matthew. I know I am being foolish, but I can't help it. This was the right one--I know it was. There will never be another like it."

"Hey now, Honey, don't take it so hard. I realize you are disappointed. I admit I am too, but we will look for something else when the time is right...that is, if you will still want to. After all, we hadn't planned on looking for anything to buy in the first place. We just happened upon it. There will be another," Matthew said, trying to convince himself, as well as Amy.

Despondently, the couple quietly got into their car and began their trip back home to New York. They drove in silence, unable to voice their feelings further about the farm they had found, and had to leave. The farm estate would have been perfect for them for many reasons. Matthew and Amy knew in their hearts, however, that they would have to accept the fact that it was not to be.

Some time later, they drove into a mass of dark and gray clouds. A cold drizzling rain began to fall, each drop onto the windshield of the car like the teardrops falling upon Amy's cheeks. Matthew and Amy's hearts echoed the gloominess surrounding them. The hum of the rubber tires on the wet pavement moaned a sorrowful tune, as the distance between the heartbroken couple and their lost dream became greater with each mile.

Chapter 8

Upon returning back home to their apartment in the big city, Matthew and Amy resumed their former routines. They forced themselves to keep busy so that they wouldn't think of what they could have had...the farm they had fallen in love with, and had to leave.

Matthew became moodier and quieter than ever in his discontent. Even though he spent more time than ever at his office, his work piled up more on his desk, unfinished. He could have delegated the workload to his office personnel, but he was oblivious to the responsibility of his company. He could not care less.

Amy, also, unhappy with everything she attempted, couldn't concentrate on her work. Her work became mechanical. For the first time, her work bored her, and at home, she moped listlessly. They rarely mentioned the farm in Kansas for it was too painful to talk about.

Sharing Matthew's frustration, she understood at last what he had long been experiencing, and she was disappointed that her idea of moving to Kansas in the promise of saving their marriage failed. She wondered if there was some other way to save their marriage, or had they lost their chance? She was at a complete loss as where to turn for answers.

Two weeks later on a Saturday morning, they sat lingering at the breakfast table sipping their morning coffee in their usual silence. Matthew scanned over the stock-market reviews in the newspaper while Amy half-heartedly mulled over the idea of re-decorating their apartment in order to occupy her mind.

The two-story white house with the wrap-a-round veranda, however, kept intruding into her schemes. She could visualize many ideas as to what she could do with the charismatic old house, and it saddened her that now she wouldn't have that chance.

The telephone rang, startling Amy out of her deep thoughts. She started to rise to go answer it, but Matthew, with a gesture of his arm, countered her action.

"Stay seated. I'll get it," Matthew said, taking a quick sip of coffee before he set down the cup. Languidly, he rose to go to answer the phone.

"Yes, sir...yes, I am. When did it happen? Yes, of course... I understand. Yes, we are indeed," Matthew said, tense astonishment paling his face, as he gripped the telephone receiver tightly in his hand.

Hearing his quick intake of breath, Amy looked up at him to see his face turn aghast, then beet-red. Standing there, blank, amazed, and much shaken, he was temporarily at a loss for words, as he listened intently to the voice at the other end of the conversation.

Seeing the seriousness on his face, a flicker of apprehension coursed through Amy, and she immediately became alarmed. She rose from the table and hurried to his side. Able to only hear his side of the telephone conversation, she became extremely worried. Waiting to hear what the call was, she stood frozen in anticipation.

"We are indeed very interested. How much? I see...No, I think we can manage that," Matthew said, as he began fidgeting nervously.

Amy was near panic. She couldn't wait another minute. She had to know what was happening. "Matthew, who is it? What is wrong?"

Matthew was too occupied with what was being said at the other end of the conversation to answer her. Gesturing for her to not ask right then, he turned back to the phone conversation. There was much more to discuss and questions to ask.

"What would we have to do? How soon? Can you make the arrangements? That sounds fine. We will try to get a flight out today. Yes, please. Thank you very much for calling. Yes, we will, and thanks again," Matthew said, gradually regaining his composure from his astonishment of what he had heard.

With a tight expression on his face, he stared at the telephone before returning it to its cradle. He turned to face Amy who was still standing impatiently at his side, half in anticipation, and half in dread to hear what had happened.

"What...what is it? Who was it that called? Matthew, you are frightening me. What happened? Don't keep me in suspense. Speak to me."

Matthew stood transfixed, stunned beyond words. He turned slowly to face Amy, not knowing how to begin.

"Amy...Honey," he began, swallowing hard. He stared at his wife for a moment before he could speak further. Then his words began tumbling out. "How quickly can you be packed and ready to go? I have to call the office to make arrangements, and you will have to reschedule your appointments. What else will we have to do? I can't think. Oh, I have to call the airlines. We don't have much time. We will have to hurry."

Hurry? Whatever do you mean, Matthew? Where are we going...and why?" Amy, asked, practically shouting, for she was totally bewildered. "Is it your parents? Oh, my God, it is your parents. You did say 'arrangements'. Did something happen to one of them...or both? Don't just stand there, Matthew. Tell me what happened."

Before Amy realized what had happened, Matthew quickly swung her off her feet into his arms, and began to spin her about the room, showering her face with kisses.

"No, Sweetheart, it isn't my parents. They are okay," he answered. Between every other word, he planted kisses on her shoulders, neck, and face. "It is unbelievable. You'll never believe what happened. I never expected it myself."

"Matthew, put me down this instant, and tell me what in the world you are talking about," Amy demanded. Totally bewildered by his conduct, she tried to break away from his embrace.

When Matthew at last released her, she looked at him in astonishment when she saw his beaming face. He threw back his head and let out a great peal of laughter. She stared at him with her eyes open wide, thinking he had indeed gone mad.

"Everything is fine, Amy. In fact, everything is wonderful."

Relief washing over her upon hearing his words of assurance, she began to breathe easier even though she was exasperated with him for keeping her in suspense.

"Matthew, don't keep me in suspense. Please tell me what this is all about. You frightened me half to death."

"My dear wife, are you ready for this? You will not believe this, but here goes. We are going back to Kansas," he announced, indicating the significance of what he was saying by grasping her arms with exuberance.

"What? Kansas?" she asked, almost shouting. "Matthew, don't tease me. What do you mean? Why would we be going back, except going to your parents? We had only been there, and they were fine then."

"I'm not teasing you, believe me. I am serious, and no, it's not my parents. Let me explain, Hon."

"Please do. I can't take this suspense any longer. Why are we going back to Kansas so soon after we've just been there? I don't want to be reminded--"

"It's okay, Amy. That was Harry Deakins, the realtor in Spring Hill, on the phone."

"What did he want? If it's about another farm, I don't want it. I don't want to go through that again."

"The farm--our farm--is back on the market. Amy, it is still for sale. Mr. Deakins learned today that the contract on the property is null and void, and he called to give us first chance in buying the farm."

Amy's mouth dropped open. She stared at Matthew in utter astonishment, unsure she had heard correctly. She didn't know whether to laugh or cry.

"I...I can't believe it, Matt. Is it really true? Or is this some sick joke? If it is, it is the cruelest thing you could do."

"Darling, it is very true. I would never joke about this," Matthew answered, smiling with intense pleasure.

"I am stunned beyond words, but how...why? I don't understand," she said, thoroughly confused. "Please explain it to me."

"As it turns out, the purchase contract was contingent upon the purchaser securing a loan, and his loan application was rejected. Do you know what that means, Amy? The farm is going to be <u>ours</u>. That is...if you still want it."

"*If* I still want it? Oh, yes, Matt...Yes, I do." It was the most incredible news she had ever heard. Her heart beating rapidly, she tried to absorb all he was telling her. Her head was spinning recklessly.

"Hurry and get packed, Amy. We will have to leave right away. I told Mr. Deakins we would come today. I need to go call the airlines."

Amy tried to think rationally, as she dashed from the room. It was all happening much too quickly. There was so much to do and so little time. She could not think of what to do first. She had to pack. Then she would have to call Chrissie's nanny. It entered her mind that it would have been nice to have taken Chrissie with them this time, but she knew there wasn't time enough to make the necessary preparations.

"What will I wear? Oh, we must hurry," she said to no one in particular before she called out to Matthew, "Hurry, Matthew. Please hurry."

Chapter 9

Amy slept peacefully with happy dreams of their new life, and of the beautiful farmhouse that was now their own. She was content in the knowledge that with their hard work and determination they were well on their way to accomplishing their goals. She and Matthew were proud of their accomplishments, and rightfully so, for they had worked assiduously during the last few months to make the farm estate truly theirs.

After moving into their new home, Matthew and Amy spent the remainder of the autumn enthusiastically and diligently cleaning up the property. Amy learned how to use the paintbrush, painting anything and everything in sight. She wallpapered and hung new curtains and draperies, while Matthew refinished the floors and woodwork.

Amy searched through catalogues for the perfect accessories for her perfect house. She had a blast. It was a thousand fold more enjoyable than anything she had ever done during her profession as an interior designer in New York, because this was their own.

The sounds of hammering and sawing were constant while Matthew made numerous repairs to the house and outbuildings. They worked together tidying the yard and pruning the shrubs.

By nightfall, they were exhausted, but happy. They would sit back to relax, satisfied with what they had accomplished for that day. Looking forward to each new day, they would discuss their ideas and make their plans of what they would do next.

Their first Christmas in the country was the most fantastic Christmas they had ever had. Snow fell as if on cue to make the day complete. Matthew and Amy joyously introduced Chrissie to snowball fighting while building a huge snowman. Chrissie delighted in making snow angels. After opening their gifts, the family basked in front of the fireplace singing carols and roasting marshmallows.

Then along came the spring with spring plowing and planting, and cattle grazing in the greening meadows. By the time the season ended, the farm estate looked like a breathtaking scene straight from an oil painting, or much like a brilliantly colored centerfold inside of <u>Country</u> magazine. They couldn't have been happier. They felt nothing could ever take that happiness away from them.

#

Dreaming of their achievements, Amy slept serenely, a hint of a smile playing upon her lips. She was content and happy until she suddenly tensed.

Something threatening...dark and sinister...began to invade Amy's dream world while she slept. She began to toss and turn, and her pillow became drenched from sweat, as she fought through the cobwebs of nightmare-filled sleep. Opening her disoriented eyes, she came back to reality. Some sixth sense brought her fully awake. Amy sat up quickly, feeling that all was not right. She listened with bewilderment, not hearing anything abnormal.

That was it! Suddenly, she realized what was wrong. It was much too quiet. A chill black silence surrounded her. All she could hear was the thumping of her heart. Apprehension coursed through her body. Something had told her...but what was it? *It was a feeling...*_____ With a keen ear, she listened attentively for any sound.

Chrissie!

Amy leaped from the bed and ran frantically to the nursery. Only when she was at the child's bedside did she start breathing normally once again. Chrissie was sleeping peacefully, her small chest rising and falling in a normal relaxed rhythm.

Turning, Amy dashed from the nursery searching for a clue of what could have caused her uneasiness. Searching throughout the house, she couldn't find anything that warranted concern--except for the uncanny stillness. She rushed to the door to continue her search, the dreadful feeling remaining with her like a dark cloud hovering overhead.

Amy stepped outdoors and looked about. There was a slight breeze stirring the clear late afternoon sky with a few wispy cirrus clouds drifting lazily across the horizon. Everything appeared to be normal, except it was much quieter than when she had gone inside to take her nap. She noticed the birds were silent, which was unusual. Even the cicadas had hushed. The silence was eerie.

Becoming increasingly uneasy, she looked about. Her anxiety turning into panic, a cold knot churned her stomach.

Matthew!

She looked toward the barnyard where he had been working earlier. He was nowhere to be seen. The blue shirt he had earlier removed and hung on the rail post was still there. Thinking something indeed had happened to her husband, she ran flying down the porch steps and through the gate toward the corral. The foreboding that something horrible had happened, or was about to happen, was growing stronger.

"Matthew," she shouted, her eyes darting around as she searched for her husband. "Matthew, where are you?"

Amy noticed that his old pickup truck was still behind the barn partially hidden out of full range. The garage door was closed; therefore, she assumed that their car was still parked inside. Besides, she knew Matthew wouldn't have left without letting her know of his intentions.

She called his name repeatedly, but always with no response. Fearing that Matthew must have been hurt--or worse--she raced to the corral. Unmindful of the gate and her physical condition, she was ready to climb over the rail when Matthew, finally hearing her frantic calls, came out of the barn with a puzzled, yet concerned, expression on his face.

"Amy, what's wrong? What is it?" he asked, as he leaped over the rails and ran to her side. "What's the matter, Sweetheart? You are as pale as a ghost."

"Thank goodness, you're all right. I was scared out of my mind," Amy said, tears of relief welling in her eyes. "I was afraid something had happened to you."

Matthew clasped her trembling body in his arms before putting her away from him to ask, observing her closely, "Tell me what's wrong. You are shaking like a leaf. Why would you think something had happened to me? I was only in the barn cleaning out the stalls. Amy, are sure you are all right?"

"No...Yes. I don't know. I...Matthew, something is wrong. Something is going to happen," Amy answered, her voice rising in near hysteria.

"Whoa now, Honey. Tell me what is upsetting you," Matthew said, reaching for his shirt and putting it on, as he tried to comprehend what she was saying. "What is this all about?"

Amy's words gushed out in an unintelligible babble."Somethingawfulisabouttohappen. Ihadadreamitwasawarning. Wehavetoleavenowhurry."

"Honey, slow down. I don't understand a word you are saying. Take a deep breath, and tell me what it is."

Obeying him, she swallowed hard, taking several deep breaths until she was able to repeat what she had said. Frantic with the imminent danger of which she was certain, she stammered, "I...I...am...scared, Matthew."

"I see that you are. Come on, Honey, everything is fine. Please calm down and tell me about it."

Trying to steady her paranoia, Matthew gathered Amy in his arms, but her fear was growing greater with every moment. Breaking away from his grip, Amy clutched his arm and tried to pull him with her.

"Please hurry," Amy pleaded, while tugging desperately on his arm. "We must go. We have to get away from here."

"Go where? What would we be running from?" Matthew asked as he tried to get a perspective on what was occurring.

With her eyes wide with fear, Amy began thrashing around looking...searching...for whatever was so evil they had to escape. "We have to leave while we still have time. I will get Chrissie. We will leave, but we have to hurry."

Matthew quickly restrained her from rushing to the house to get Chrissie. She tried to resist him, but he wouldn't let her go.

"Stop, Amy. Calm yourself. We aren't going anywhere until you explain to me why you are being hysterical. I don't know what is going on, but this is going too far. This isn't good for you, or for the baby."

Matthew was frustrated with her, yet he couldn't stop worrying about her. It was unlike Amy to be irrational like that, and he was confused as what he should do.

"Listen to me, Matthew. We have to get away from here. I was sleeping. Something woke me...a warning...something awful is going to happen--and soon," Amy said in panic, trying to make him understand, as she grasped the front of Matthew's shirt with her fists.

Upon hearing her frantic explanation, Matthew studied the surroundings around them. He couldn't see anything unusual, except for his wife's strange behavior. It troubled him deeply when he saw that her blue eyes were intense with a dark depth of fear. He knew he had to convince Amy somehow that nothing was going to happen to them.

He thought what she had related to him was too preposterous to take seriously, and it had been only a dream, a very bad nightmare. He was positive she was over emotional because of her pregnancy, and he was concerned that it was not good for her.

Gripping her shoulders firmly, he said, "Look at me and listen. You have to get a hold of yourself. Think of the baby, if nothing else."

"No, you don't understand. How many times do I have to tell you? Something terrible is going to happen--and soon. Do you hear me, Matthew? We are in danger."

"Amy, you must listen to me," Matthew said, trying to reason with her while gently shaking her. He was quickly losing his patience with her. "Nothing is going to happen to you, me, or to Chrissie."

"How do you know that? You don't know. I am telling you, we are not safe here," she answered, getting aggravated with him. "Why can't you believe me? Please believe me, Matthew."

"Come on, Honey, it's all right. You just had a nightmare."

"No, it wasn't," Amy snapped back, beating her fists on his chest.

"Come here," Matthew said soothingly while he tried to pull her tightly into his arms. He quickly saw he was fighting a losing battle of convincing her that there was nothing of which to be frightened. He attempted to take her in his arms again, but she would not be persuaded.

"Oh, I wish we had never come here."

"Amy! No, you are just upset. You don't mean that," Matthew said, stunned to hear her declaration, and tried to tell himself that she was only panicking. She was not being herself.

Out of anger and desperation, she pushed Matthew away from her. As she turned away from him, she gave up trying to persuade him that there was danger. Facing the southwest and beyond the tree line, Amy stood forlornly and watched in defeat, waiting to see whatever it was that was so terrible that she could not name.

"It is something dark and horrible like...a storm...or a..." Amy said distantly in a low voice, but unable to continue. In her whirling mind, she tried to remember something she was supposed to remember, but couldn't.

Feeling powerless, Matthew could only stand silently by and gaze at his agonizing wife. He felt more afraid for her than he had ever felt before.

"Oh, I don't know," Amy said in her confusion, her voice rising to a shrill, yet she continued to scan the sky.

"Amy, don't do this to yourself."

"It was a warning of some kind. I know it was a warning--but about what?"

"Honey, don't do this to yourself."

Suddenly, Amy grew quiet. Her tears subsided, as she stood transfixed toward the horizon. "Matthew, look," she said, pointing toward an area between the trees where one could see the azure blue sky and the giant green meadow meet. "Isn't it...Oh, Matthew, it *is* coming."

A glazed look of despair spread over her face, as she stumbled forward to stare in waiting silence.

Matthew rushed to her side to see what it was that she was seeing and frightening her. All he could see in the clear blue sky, however, was a slight darkening appearing on the horizon.

"Honey, it's only a cloud gathering. That's all it is," Matthew answered calmly, relieved that it was nothing more, but he still was puzzled about Amy's torment. Placing an arm around Amy's shoulder, he continued, "With a little luck, we will get some rain out of it. Heaven knows we do need it, but the weather forecast didn't indicate that we were going to have any precipitation."

"Stop it," Amy said, reacting angrily as she shrugged his arm away without taking her gaze from the harmless-looking cloud that was slowly appearing on the horizon. "Please don't try to pacify me. I feel…No, I know there is more to it than it being only a rain cloud."

"Amy, I don't understand you. I've never seen you this way before."

"I'm sorry, Matt, I don't understand it either. I cannot explain, except I am frightened, and I am frightened for you and Chrissie," Amy said, trying to explain.

"What were you dreaming at the time? Tell me what happened," Matthew asked, trying to make some sense from what she was saying.

"All I know is that something is going to happen. I don't know how or why, but the feeling is getting stronger. It was in my dream, but I don't know what it was. Please, you have to believe me."

"I do believe you. I understand that you are frightened of something, but I'd like to know what it is. What could be so terrible that would make you panic like this?"

She didn't answer him. She felt it was pointless to, for she, herself, didn't have the answers. Her head bowed, her body slumped in despair, as a silent grief overwhelmed her.

Gathering her into arms again, he held her snugly. This time she didn't shrug off his touch, but leaned against him in defeat. Matthew didn't know what else to say or do. He had pleaded with her; he had bullied her; he had pacified her, but nothing he did could change her mind, nor console her. All he could do was to hold her tightly.

After all, what more could he say to her that he hadn't already said? The couple stood there silently keeping their vigil on the sky and on that one solitary cloud slowly separating itself from the horizon.

As they watched, the darkening cloud began to grow while it stretched across the sky, gaining life in its being. The cloud had a slight greenish hue intermingled with its dark and eerie grayness as it continued to darken the late afternoon sky.

"It is coming," Amy whispered in a voice of doom.

"Amy, please stop worrying about it. Don't do this to yourself. The cloud doesn't look that bad. We have seen worse. It is probably just a front coming through. We, more than likely, won't even get any rain from it. There is nothing to fear, you'll see. Please relax, Darling."

As he spoke with assurance that they were in no danger, he noticed the cloud growing before his eyes. As he gazed at the formation, he became more aware of the speed with which it was approaching--and the color. Matthew had never before seen a rain cloud with such a greenish hue.

Before their eyes, the cloud began to look fearsome as it lengthened like an ominous green hand with its wispy fingers stretching, reaching out to grasp anything in its way.

The wind grew still into a deadly calm. The atmosphere became heavy, causing Matthew and Amy difficulty in breathing. Even the sounds of the late afternoon had stilled to a deadly silence as the cloud grew nearer. There was an eeriness to the calm, as they waited and watched.

Her nerves tensing, Amy bit her lip, and clinched her hands until her nails entered her palms. She had never been more frightened as she was now.

Watching the approaching cloud drawing nearer, it reminded Matthew of a cloud once before...the tornado that had taken his family's home. It brought back all the awful memories of the fears, and the destruction. The same kind of fingers. Shaking his head in denial, he thought surely not again.

Reconsidering the severity of the cloud that was approaching in their direction, he thought of Amy and Chrissie's safety, and that maybe, they should seek shelter. He couldn't risk taking a chance of endangering their lives.

It occurred to Matthew that if they needed to, they could seek shelter in the old storm cellar in their backyard, but he abruptly dismissed the idea. The cellar was crumbling apart, leaving cracks and holes, allowing snakes and rodents to enter, making it unsafe to use. Making it unsafe, also, was the rotted wooden door of the entrance, and the steps going down into the interior. Matthew hadn't had the time to repair or replace the storm cellar, making it definitely unsuitable for their shelter.

Coming to a quick decision, Matthew said, "Maybe we should leave to go somewhere else for shelter, just to be on the safe side."

Heaving a sigh of relief that Matthew had finally agreed to leave, Amy answered, "Thank you, Matt. We can't stay here."

Having made the decision to leave, he sprang into action. "All right, Amy, if we're going, let's go. This is now coming quickly. Get Chrissie while I get the car, and, Amy…It might be best to hurry."

Matthew turned on his heels and headed for the garage. He cast his eyes to the approaching storm, and worried about the unusual formations growing with it. He was quickly concluding that this was something more than an ordinary rainstorm cloud. Yet, he denied that this cloud had anything to with Amy's dream.

It was too absurd.

Chapter 10

Matthew didn't have to warn Amy to hurry. As Amy raced to the house, she felt as if her legs could not travel fast enough. She dashed through the door, letting the screen door slam shut behind her. Just as she started toward Chrissie's bedroom, Chrissie emerged from her room dragging her favorite blue blanket behind her.

"Me through sleeping," Chrissie said in a matter-of-factly manner to her mother.

"There's my sweet girl. I saw that you had a nice nap," Amy said, giving her a quick hug while she reminded herself not to frighten the child. "Come, Sweetheart, we are going to go bye-bye for a little while."

"Are we going to Grandma and Grandpa's?"

"No, Sweetie, not today," Amy replied, wishing what was occurring at that moment was as simple as going to visit Matthew's parents who lived upstate.

Amy started to lift Chrissie up into her arms, but the child resisted and began to cry. "Me want my dolly. Dolly want to go bye-bye too, Mommy."

"All right, but wait right here," Amy answered, as she relented impatiently, knowing that valuable time was being lost. They had to leave before it was too late. "I will get your dolly, but you have to wait right here. Okay?"

"Okay, Mommy. Can I draw you and Daddy a picture? I like to color."

"That would be nice, but not now. I will be right back. Just don't wander off, Chrissie. Stay right here while I get your doll."

Amy dashed into the nursery and snatched up the horrid doll, knowing it would have been useless to try to convince Chrissie to leave the doll behind, as it was her overall favorite doll.

In her frantic hurry to return to Chrissie, Amy stumbled against the side table in the darkened hallway. She was only slightly aware that the motion knocked a framed family portrait of Matthew, Chrissie, and herself to the floor. She hesitated a second to sadly glance down at the precious portrait with their faces smiling up at her from behind the broken glass. Realizing that too much time had been wasted, she couldn't take the time to stop to retrieve the portrait from the floor to return it upon the table.

She was completely unaware that the incident of the portrait with the broken glass could very well have been a bad omen for her and her happy family. After dashing to the living room where she had left the small child, Amy gasped, widening her eyes in alarm. Chrissie was nowhere in sight.

"Oh my God, Chrissie, where are you? Please come out wherever you are. This is no time to be playing." Amy screamed the words in an inner frightening turmoil that was akin to panic, knowing that they had to get away from there while there was time.

The storm was almost upon them, and the afternoon light was quickly fading. They didn't have much time left for their escape. Frantically, Amy spun around searching the room, but the child was not there. She could not think rationally. She didn't know what to do, or where to begin searching for the child.

Amy called Chrissie's name repeatedly, but the child never answered her anxious calls...nor did she come.

"Where can she be?" Amy cried hysterically. "We have to get away from here." She rushed frantically from room to room in search of her missing daughter.

Meanwhile, Matthew was waiting impatiently near their red convertible with his eyes cast upon the approaching storm. He wondered why Amy was taking so much time in coming with Chrissie, when earlier she had been in a frenzy to leave.

Deciding he should go warn her to hurry, he ran to the house, leaping up the porch steps, two rungs at a time, calling her name. Amy, wide-eyed with fright, clutched Chrissie's blanket tightly to her body, as she met him at the door.

"There you are, Amy, we had better--"

"Chrissie is gone. I can't find her anywhere," Amy interrupted, fear, stark and vivid, glittered in her eyes. "She just vanished."

Stunned, Matthew cast his eyes anxiously around the room, expecting the child to appear at any time. He felt it certainly was bad timing for her to wander off when it was crucial for them to leave as soon as possible to escape the building storm.

"She wasn't in her bed?"

"No, we were coming. She was right here. I went back to Chrissie's room to get her doll. When I returned, she wasn't here. I looked everywhere for her but I can't find her," Amy answered, wringing her hands in anguish. "Matthew, where is she? Where could she have gone? We have to find her."

"Don't worry, Honey, we'll find her. We'll search again. She has to be somewhere around here."

Matthew ran from the room to begin his search while Amy went in another direction to search elsewhere. They searched everywhere. They looked behind the sofa, behind chairs, and under tables. They searched under the beds, in closets, and everywhere else they could possibly think of looking.

Amy was frantic with worry, as she tried to think where Chrissie normally played, but every place she looked, Chrissie was not there. She wondered how Chrissie could just simply vanish.

When Matthew rejoined Amy after his own unsuccessful search throughout the entire house, he could only shake his head. The storm was quickly approaching, and their tiny daughter was missing at the most inopportune time. He couldn't help but wonder why this was happening to them. And why now, of all times?

"Matthew, outside! We haven't looked outside. Chrissie may have--"

Matthew didn't waste another second. He ran through the kitchen and to the back door. Amy and Matthew had failed to notice during their frantic search for Chrissie that the kitchen door was ajar, and the screen door was unlatched.

Sighing with enormous relief, he presumed she had wandered outside and would be in the confines of the fenced backyard. He knew Chrissie couldn't have ventured far. The gate had been always kept securely latched to prevent the inquisitive child from leaving the safety of the backyard.

He ran out the door and down the wooden porch steps to the backyard with Amy close at his heels, silently praying that they would find Chrissie in time, and that she would be all right. Calling out Chrissie's name repeatedly, Matthew searched the small enclosed backyard. Not seeing her anywhere, he ran searching in and behind everything. Still, there was no sign of her.

"Chrissie, where are you? Come out from where you are hiding," Matthew called out impatiently, yet becoming worried about her whereabouts. Scanning the darkened sky, he knew they would have to find her before it was too late.

"She's not here either," Amy said in dismay, with terror written on her face. "Something terrible has happened to our Chrissie. What are we going to do? Where is she? We must find her. Please, Matthew, find our baby girl."

"She has to be somewhere around here. She couldn't have left the yard for the gate is still latched. Now think, Amy. Where are her favorite places? Where does she do when she isn't playing in her playhouse or sandbox?"

Amy thought about all the different places where Chrissie liked to play...the playhouse that Matthew had lovingly built, behind the enormous oak tree, the swing hanging from a limb of the oak tree, the sandbox, under the porch...

"The porch! Matthew, look under the porch. I forgot that she likes to play under there."

The words were scarcely out of Amy's mouth before Matthew dashed to the back porch. Dropping to the ground on all four limbs, he peered anxiously into the dim and cool crawl space underneath the wooden porch.

He breathed a huge sigh of relief to find Chrissie contentedly sitting there on the cool earthen ground totally absorbed at coloring in her coloring book. Shattered on the ground around her was an array of crayons.

"Here she is, Amy. I found her."

"Oh, thank God. Is she all right?"

"Yes," Matthew answered, smiling with relief. "It appears that our little girl is quite okay."

"Look what I make, Daddy. See? Me color pretty picture," Chrissie said, proudly holding up her coloring book to show her father the childish scrawls on the page.

"Yes, Sweetheart, it is pretty, but it is time to go now."

Reluctantly, Chrissie laid down the book and the crayons that she held in her chubby little fingers and went to her father. He reached out to grasp her and then scooped her into his protective arms.

Watching breathlessly, and clutching Chrissie's blanket and doll tightly to her, Amy eyes filled with tears of relief that their baby girl was all right. She couldn't bear the thought of anything terrible happening to their precious daughter.

"Come on, Amy, we need to hurry. It looks as if we don't have a minute to spare for that storm is starting to look fierce," Matthew urged. "Let's go."

They rushed out the gate and to the car. Matthew literally shoved Amy into the seat. Dropping Chrissie into her lap and slamming the car door shut, he ran around the vehicle to the driver's side and jumped inside to begin their escape from the ominous-looking storm cloud.

"The cloud is becoming awfully dark and ugly," Amy remarked. She was astounded how large and severe the storm looked since she had gone into the house, and during the time they had searched for Chrissie.

The vengeful storm was bearing down upon them. The wind returned, beginning with a low rumbling sound before turning into a raging roar. The dark, ominous grayish-green mass continued gaining its strength to lay claim on anything in its path. It would have no mercy on anything--or anyone.

Chapter 11

The increasing gusts of wind blew dust and debris, obscuring the McCormack's view, as they turned out from the long driveway onto the main country road. The forceful wind vehemently rocked the vehicle making it difficult for Matthew to maintain control.

The ominous storm cloud darkened the late afternoon sky as it roared and stretched low across the horizon. The treetops whipped back and forth, and the grass in the meadows and along the roadside flattened and shivered.

In their frantic escape from the storm, Matthew and Amy were uncertain as to where they would go. They only knew that their lives depended on somehow outrunning the vicious storm. While they had been engrossed in escaping the storm as quickly as possible, Matthew failed to heed the danger of traveling at such a great speed on the loosely graveled road. Both, Matthew and Amy's only thought was of getting away from the path of the storm.

Nor did they notice their neighbor, Lizzie Thornton, as she stood on the front porch of her solitary house watching them as they sped by.

Amy kept turning about in her seat to keep vigil on the ominous-looking storm. She silently prayed that they would be able to overcome this catastrophic peril that appeared to be chasing them with no mercy.

Matthew, sensing the impending danger they were in, kept a watchful eye on the threatening storm through the rear-view mirror. He gripped the steering wheel, as he pressed his foot harder on the accelerator, causing dust to billow up like smoke from the tires. With the increased speed with which they were traveling and the raging storm at their backs, the terrified couple became tenser.

Amy, holding Chrissie closely as she stared at the road ahead, suddenly realized Matthew's error. Turning to him, she called out, "Matthew, we just passed the intersection. Weren't we going into town?"

By the time Amy shouted out the warning, they were already past the intersection where they were to turn off toward Spring Hill, the small rural town that was nearest to their home.

"Damn, I wasn't watching," Matthew said, aggravated with himself for not having been more observant. As they had no time to spare, he couldn't stop to reverse the car or to turn around. He had no other choice but to continue driving in the direction in which they were traveling.

"What do we do now, Matt?" Amy asked in a small frightened voice.

"I'm sorry. I should have been more careful," Matthew said. He became thoughtful for a moment until he had an idea. "Okay, we'll go on to the next intersection. If the storm doesn't veer off into another direction by then, we will turn there to detour into Spring Hill. But surely, we will outrun the storm by then."

"Do you really think we can outrun it?" Amy asked, her heart hammering with fear.

"I know you are frightened, Honey, but we will be all right."

"I wish I could be so sure...The cloud is becoming darker and look how green the sky is. It is eerie," she said, a cold chill running down her spine.

Realizing that they were in a dangerous situation, Matthew, tight-lipped, gripped the steering wheel and tried to concentrate on his driving. He had no idea where they would go, but he had to believe that with some luck they would outrun the storm. Beyond that, he couldn't imagine what they would do.

Amy, concentrating on Matthew's high rate of speed and the storm at their backs, inadvertently relaxed her hold on Chrissie, who was restlessly squirming in her lap.

Relieved to be free from her mother's tight grip, Chrissie slid from her lap and settled onto the seat between her parents. Casting her inquisitive eyes around the interior of the car, Chrissie's eyes came to rest on the car stereo. Too young to understand their plight, Chrissie didn't realize that she unfortunately chose the wrong time to reach for the knob to turn on the stereo.

In the past, her parents had often been permissive in allowing her to turn on the stereo whenever they were in the vehicle; therefore, Chrissie had no idea that today would have been definitely a bad time to turn on the music as she had previously been allowed.

With a smile on her face, the child reached with her chubby little fingers to innocently switch on the knob. The blast of loud music that came forth startled them all.

"Don't, for Pete's sake. Turn that thing off," Matthew barked with annoyance, as he turned his eyes off the road for only a split second to reach out to turn off the music.

"Matthew, watch out," Amy screamed, snatching the child back into the safety of her arms as quickly as possible.

Matthew tried desperately to regain control of the swerving vehicle, but he had been driving much too fast on the loosely-graveled road. The car skidded out of control, coming to a stop only after the front of the vehicle went off the deep embankment, the right front wheel spinning crazily in mid-air. There was a dead silence amidst the dust that engulfed the vehicle and the occupants within.

A few moments later, Matthew, the first to recover from the shocking jolt, reached toward his family with immediate concern.

"Oh, my gosh, Amy. Are you all right?" he asked, peering closely at Amy and Chrissie. He was horrified that they might have been badly injured.

Stunned from the mishap, Amy slowly became aware of her surroundings and that they had an accident. In her shocked state, she could vaguely hear Chrissie crying hysterically, but she wasn't able to concentrate in order to calm her. For the moment, all she could do was to press back into the leather seat and hold tightly onto the screaming child.

It took several moments for Amy to realize that Matthew was speaking to her. "Yes...I think so," Amy answered slowly, as his words registered in her mind. Her voice trembled, as her eyes and mind tried to focus. "But, what happened? Where are we?"

"We ran off the road, nothing serious, as long as you and Chrissie are okay."

The sound of the wailing child, along with the roar of the wind, slowly brought Amy to an awareness of what had happened.

"Oh, my gosh. The storm. I remember now. And Chrissie. Are you okay, Baby?"

Immediately, Amy began to search Chrissie over for any possible injuries, while Matthew tried to decide what he should do.

"Are the two of you all right, Amy?" Matthew asked again out of concern to his family.

Attempting to soothe the frightened child, Amy looked up toward Matthew and answered, "I'm okay, and I think Chrissie is also. She is just frightened out of her soul. Matthew, what are we going to do now?"

"I honesty don't know. I'm so sorry for letting this happen. It's all my fault. I should have been more careful." Guilt overtook him for his foolish mistake, which well could have resulted in disaster.

"Don't blame yourself. It was an accident...You couldn't help it."

"If you or Chrissie had been injured, I wouldn't have been able to forgive myself."

Glancing around their surroundings, Amy became alarmed again. The car. What if...Taking a deep breath, she had to ask. "Matthew, what about the car? Is it damaged? Oh, my God, will it run?"

"Surely, it is okay. It has to be," he replied, not sure of anything at that moment.

Worried, Matthew looked up at the now cloud-filled sky that was continuing to darken. The sunny blue of earlier being entirely obscured, he knew they would have to do something immediately.

He hurried to switch on the ignition--Nothing happened. Breathing a silent prayer, he tried again, and then again. Still, no sound came from the engine. At last, the motor coughed and sputtered until it began to run nosily. Matthew breathed a sigh of relief as he put the gear into reverse, but the car wouldn't budge. He could only guess at the damage the small vehicle had sustained.

"Dammit, why couldn't I have been more careful?" Matthew asked, pounding his fists on the steering wheel.

"We had to escape as quickly as possible, and we both were under too much pressure to concentrate on your driving, and the distraction from Chrissies' turning on the radio was a misfortune, but she's only a baby. She didn't know any better," Amy said, trying hard not place blame on any of them.

"I know. I'm sorry. I'm not placing blame on anyone," Matthew said apologetically. "I'm just angry that this had to happen now when it is so important to outrun this storm."

"What do you think is preventing the car from moving? What is wrong with it?"

"I don't have a clue. I have to take a look around outside. Maybe I will find out something," Matthew said, quickly jumping out of the vehicle and began looking over its condition. As soon as he reached the other side of the car, he immediately saw what the problem was. Unfortunately, the car was stuck on high-center, the right front wheel dangling precariously over the deep embankment.

It was definite that they had gone as far as they could. Matthew had no choice but to suggest to Amy what he knew they had to do. They couldn't stay there in the car because of the threatening storm. It was too dangerous.

"We will have to leave the car and go on by foot. Do you think you can handle it, Amy, in your condition? I'm sorry, but I see no other way."

"I suppose so, but...Matt, where are we going to go that will be safe from this storm? There is no place to go now, nor have time to get to any shelter."

"Yes, there is. I remember now that there is an abandoned building just down the road. I don't think it is very far from here, and I don't know whether it will be safe enough from the storm but right now we have no other choice. We will have to try make a run for it."

Immediately going into action, Matthew reached into the vehicle for Chrissie and wrapped her securely in her blanket. With his free hand he then helped Amy slide across the seat to exit for it was impossible for her to exit from the passenger side because of the deep embankment.

Once out of the stranded vehicle, they proceeded to move down the road on foot until Amy came to an immediate stop when she remembered Chrissie's doll. She knew, without a doubt, that there was no way in the world they could leave behind Chrissie's most-loved doll. It flashed through her mind that this was the second time within minutes that she had to retrieve that wretched doll.

Not given a choice, Amy had to go back for it for Chrissie's sake. While Matthew waited with Chrissie in his arms, Amy turned and ran back to the vehicle to retrieve the doll from the floorboard where it had dropped when the accident occurred.

When Amy caught back up with Matthew and Chrissie, she noticed the wind had once again calmed, which appeared to be more menacing than the potent wind.

The sky glowed with a strange eerie green color, as the dark ferocious-looking cloud hovered over the threesome. The cloud with its spewing fingers continued moving, creating various twisting shapes at random.

A shudder going through her body, Amy continued to feel threatened by the strong current of foreboding. She wondered why the storm doesn't pass, and why did it continued to follow them, as if to--urge them onward.

Matthew was aware that they had lost too much time. They would have to hurry if they were to make it to the shelter before the storm took its toll on them.

They hastened down the deserted country road, Matthew in the lead with his blanketed burden, and Amy close at his heels. Constantly glancing back at her, he was concerned about Amy's delicate condition; therefore, he tried to slow his pace for her to be able to keep up with him. Shortly after they began their journey by foot, the wind once again returned in full force, pushing and whipping at its victims backs with all its fury, making their plight more difficult with each step they took. They both became weak with exhaustion from fighting the fierce wind, along with the stress of their ordeal.

Becoming exhausted and out of breath, and feeling she couldn't take another step, Amy kept glancing back over her shoulder at the storm. Being in a fearful hurry, and not watching her step, Amy stumbled on the loose gravel. Falling to the ground, she scraped her arms and knees. The palms of her hands bled from the abrasive gravel when she tried to stop her fall with her hands.

"Matthew, wait," she screamed. "Help me. I can't go on," she said in desperation, hot tears flowing down her cheeks.

Unaware that Amy had fallen, Matthew turned when he heard her plea for help and rushed back to her, shouting against the violent wind, "Are you all right?" Not waiting for her answer, he awkwardly tried with his free arm to help Amy rise to her feet. "Come on, Honey, let me help you. We have to hurry."

"I can't, Matthew. I can't go any farther."

"Yes, you can, you have to. It's not far now, we're almost there. Hurry and get up. It's just a little farther," Matthew answered over the roar of the wind.

The ferocious wind threatened to tear the blanketed bundle from Matthew's arms as he struggled against the wind to help Amy rise to her feet. Regretfully, he didn't have time be concerned about Amy's injuries, or administer first aid to her. Their lives depended on getting to the safety of the old building in time, and there was no time to spare.

"Look, there it is, Amy," Matthew said excitedly, as he pointed up the road.

Ahead to the right of the road in an overgrown meadow sat an old deserted building that was partially obscured by weeds and brush. Anyone who was unfamiliar with the area would not have noticed the building unless they had known of its existence.

Casting her eyes toward where he pointed, she scrutinized the old structure. Not having noticed it before, she was surprised at its existence; however, she was glad it was there. The old building looked like a castle to her, and gave her new hope and encouragement.

Helping her to her feet, Matthew placed his arm around her waist to give support to her wearied unsteadiness. Urging her forward, they dashed for the gate opening of the long-neglected barb-wired fence.

Placing the bundled child into Amy's arms, he unfastened the rusty wire loop that fastened the barb-wired gate. It was evident that the rusty gate hadn't been used for quite some time.

Lowering the upper portion of the gate, Matthew helped her step over to the other side. Retrieving Chrissie from her arms, he propelled Amy forward through the overgrown meadow.

With the storm urging them forward into the unknown, they dashed with renewed strength for the safety of the old deserted building.

Only later would Matthew and Amy realize that they would have to face far greater perils than what they had just survived-- far greater than they had ever thought possible--or imaginable.

Chapter 12

As the trio approached the shelter, the wind grew calmer. The dark vengeful storm with its evil fingers, however, continued following its victims as it stretched and reached....

"I noticed this building last winter when the grass had turned brown and laid. You could see it easily then," Matthew said, as they fought their way through the overgrown weeds to the entrance of the abandoned building.

"Thank God we are almost there. I don't think I'm able to go much farther," Amy said, breathlessly. Watchful of where she was stepping, she tried hard not to think about what varmints might be hiding among the weeds and brush. Instead, she needed to concentrate on them reaching the safety of the shelter. She kept repeating to herself, "It's just a little farther. Just a little farther. We can make it, we will make it."

Panting laboriously, Amy and Matthew were weak with exhaustion as they approached the building that was to provide safety for them. With great relief, they reached the entrance, and realized that, unfortunately, their relief was short-lived.

They stopped. In utter dismay, a sob erupted from Amy's throat and Matthew grimaced in anguish, as they saw that they were still far from being safe from the storm. Standing before them was a heavily barred barricade that protected the thick weathered wooden door, making it impossible for Amy and Matthew to enter the vacated building that was to be their refuge from the storm.

Tears coming to her eyes, Amy said in desperation, "No, it can't be. We can't get in."

"We will, Honey. There'll be a way."

Staring at the ominous dark cloud that was hovering over them, Amy was sure that they had finally run out of time. "How, Matthew? My God, we are doomed."

In determination, Matthew thrust Chrissie into Amy's arms and began pulling with all his might to free the bars. After struggling to dislodge the bars, Matthew, using all his strength, was finally able to free the bars from the door, but only to find the door to his dismay, had been secured with a sturdy chained iron lock attached to the door latch.

Terrified, Amy looked at Matthew for some kind of assurance, but there was none when she saw his ashen face.
She felt they were defeated. They had almost reached safety, yet another obstacle confronted them. She wanted to deny that this was really happening to them, but she couldn't. Before them was the thick wooden door under lock and chain that prevented them from the shelter they desperately needed.

"NOooo, no," Amy wailed. "We won't be able to get inside. We'll never make it. We're all going to die."

Matthew saw that Amy was panicking. He knew the only hope of saving himself and his precious family was to find a way of getting inside the old building for whatever protection it would give.

"Hold on, Sweetheart. There has to be a way. I have to find something that is strong enough to use to break through the lock," he said, searching for a clue as what he could use.

Upon noticing the heavy bars that he had pulled off the door lying on the ground, he found his answer. "Here, this should work. I'll have it open soon."

"Thank God. Oh, please hurry. There's not another minute to spare. The storm is right over us."

Matthew, snatching up one of the bars, struck with a strong thrust, at the lock and door until, at last, the lock and latch broke free, and the heavy door gave way, bursting open.

In their haste to get inside to safety, they stumbled through the door, and fell onto the cool and damp earthen floor in the dark interior of what was to become their fortress.

Recovering first, Matthew leaped to his feet and said, "Wait here, Amy. It is so dark in here. Let me check around first to see if it is safe enough to wait the storm out here." It occurred to him that they really had no other choice but to remain there regardless of the building's condition, but he chose to remain silent. Amy was frightened enough.

Obeying Matthew, Amy fearfully waited by the door with Chrissie clinging to her leg. As her eyes adjusted to the dim light, she surveyed the room around her nervously.

It was dark in the room, the only light available sifting in through a small window covered with iron bars high out of reach. The windowpane, if there had ever been one, was gone.

She observed that the bare room was large with a high ceiling; the walls were of aged wood siding that was covered with a thin coat of plaster. Through the years, patches of the plaster had peeled away from the surface, revealing the bare wood.

The floor was earthen, damp, and cool from the lack of sunlight. A strong odor of mustiness in the long-closed interior of the vacated building proved that it had been vacant for a long while.

From where Amy stood surveying the room, she could see that there was a doorway leading, supposedly, into an adjoining room.

"What is this place, Matthew? It can't be a house. It is kind of spooky," she called out to Matthew. Nevertheless, she was grateful that the structure was there, knowing that it could very well save their lives.

"I don't know. This could have been a grain storage at some time, or some type of barn," Matthew answered, as he began searching the room. "Hey, we're in luck. Here's a lantern."

Matthew reached for the dusty kerosene lantern that had been left hanging on the wall. Satisfied that there was enough fuel left in the reservoir of the lantern, he dug into his jeans pocket for his cigarette lighter. Matthew breathed a sigh of relief when his fingers found the familiar metal in his pocket.

After having lit the lantern, Matthew searched the room looking for any evil foes there might be. A rodent darted away upon his intrusion. Matthew didn't see anything else that would be disturbing, except for a couple of rodents scurrying to hide, some small animal carcasses, and rodent droppings.

Noticing the door to the adjoining room, he immediately went to investigate.

"Matthew, please be careful," Amy called out to him, as he cautiously entered the second room to continue his search.

Once inside, he found that this room contained a small window much like the one in the other room, which gave some light into this room. Finding another lantern hanging on the wall, he took it from its hook and lit the wick before hanging it back on the wall.

The light from the lantern, along with the one he held, emitted enough light to show that this room was similar to the outer room, except it was narrower. Along the narrow end of one wall was a long wooden bench supported on sturdy legs. Other than the bench, the room was empty.

Satisfied with his inspection, Matthew returned to his anxiously awaiting family in the outer room. He felt confident that the building would be secure enough and was anxious to assure them that this place would be safe in which to wait out the storm.

"You can come on in. Everything looks okay to me. We shall be safe here," Matthew said with assurance.

"Thank goodness," Amy answered, sighing in relief with renewed courage. She advanced with caution a few feet into the room from where she had waited with Chrissie clutching to her leg, and gazed about. This not being the time or place to let Chrissie wander away, Amy kept a tight grip on her hand to keep her close by her side.

Hastening to the entrance, Matthew made a final inspection of the ominous and persistent storm that was hovering outside before he slammed the heavy door shut. For added support, he hoisted a thick wooden beam that he had found lying in a pile of boards in a corner of the room, and braced it solidly against the door.

"That should now be sturdy enough if the wind gets any stronger. Now, we just need to wait out the storm," he said with confidence.

Hurrying to where Amy and Chrissie waited, he gave Chrissie a huge hug, then took Amy into his arms and held her closely. As Matthew held Amy, he felt her trembling body slowly relax against him while Chrissie, still frightened by her surroundings, clung to their legs.

It was then that he remembered Amy's earlier fall. "Are you feeling all right, Amy, and what about the baby? That was quite a fall you had," Matthew asked.

"Yes, Matt, I'm okay. We're both fine. I just scraped my hands and knees," Amy answered, as she turned the palms of her hands over to inspect them for the first time since she had fallen. There was little damage to her hands except for some grime and a few remaining flecks of drying blood from the broken skin.

Matthew removed his handkerchief from his pocket and gently wiped her injured palms before he took her back into his arms. "There, you are as good as new. Now, let's enjoy our home away from home," Matthew said, smiling tenderly at Amy, as he tried to make light of their dire situation.

"Oh, Matt, it was horrible. I honestly thought we would never be able to get away from the terrible storm," she said admittedly to her husband.

As her eyes lifted to the storm's eerie glow entering through the barred window, she noticed gray shadows lurking everywhere as they slid across the ceiling and spilled down the walls. She was still somewhat apprehensive about their safety regardless of what her husband said.

"We will be free from danger here. Honey, I would never let anything harm you. I love you too much," Matthew said with tenderness into her hair.

"I know that. And I love you. We are fortunate that this building was here and that we were able to get inside. When I think about seeing those bars on the door...It is too awful to even think about."

"At least we're lucky that an abandoned place like this is as clean as it is," Matthew answered, as he released Amy and gazed around the dusty room that smelled of mustiness. "It could have been much worse."

Her eyes darting around surveying the interior, she screwed up her nose in distaste. "You call this clean? You must be kidding. Matthew, I don't know about this."

"We'll be safe here. There's nothing here to harm us, and the walls look sturdy enough to withstand the storm. It is my guess that this building has stood here vacant for many years and has withstood many storms. Besides, the storm will surely pass soon, and then we'll be able to go back home."

"I hope you are right. I never want to go through anything like that again. I was terrified we wouldn't be able to make it here in time. I have never been more frightened in my life," Amy admitted, shuttering as she stepped back into the comfort of his strong protective arms.

"After the storm passes, I will go back home after the pickup while you wait here with Chrissie. I don't want you to have to walk any further than you have to. You have already exerted yourself more than you should have in your condition."

"I am very exhausted," Amy admitted. "I don't think I could have gone any farther."

Chrissie, still hanging onto her mother, drew her attention as she whimpered, "Mommy, I'm cold, and it's dark. I don't like dark. I don't like it here. Let's go home."

The small child was frightened and confused of the flight they had taken. Now, she was frightened of the menacing dimness of the cold and shadowy interior of their new and strange surroundings.

"I know, Sweetie. I don't like it here either, and we'll go soon," Amy said, consoling Chrissie, whose large blue eyes filled with tears and slowly found their way down her chubby little cheeks.

"I wanna' go home now," Chrissie said pleadingly. "I want my dolly. Where is she?"

"Here she is, all safe and sound," her father answered, smiling at his daughter as he picked the doll up from the floor where it had dropped when they had tumbled into the darkness of the room. As he handed the favorite doll to her outstretched arms, thoughts of the storm and accident raced through his mind, causing him to ask himself whatever would he do if he ever lost his precious family.

Tucking the doll under her arm, Chrissie began rubbing her

eyes. "Mommy, I sleepy. I don't feel good," she said, her words dying away into a low murmur. "I wanna' go home."

Kneeling on the floor, Amy pulled Chrissie into the comfort of her arms. "Here, Baby, it's okay. We are safe now. We will go home soon," Amy said, saying the soothing words to herself as well as to the whimpering child. Settling Chrissie onto her lap, Amy embraced her in her
arms. In dismay, Amy looked up at Matthew.

"She is burning up with fever. She is ill. We have to do something," Amy said, alarmingly.

"We can't leave here, at least not until the storm is over. We'll have to wait it out, hopefully not for long," Matthew answered.

Stroking the child's head, and with tenderness, Amy brushed away a tendril of Chrissie's hair that had stuck to her damp face, dampened from her tears, and now with her extremely high temperature.

"Why doesn't the storm pass? It should have been over long before now," Amy asked, cradling Chrissie close in her arms, and watched the child for further developments of her illness.

"I don't know. It is strange. I've never seen a storm linger this long."

"Matthew, I think her temperature is rising. I can't stand this. We can't stay here and watch her die," Amy said in anguish, feeling Chrissie become limp in her arms.

Amy and Matthew simultaneously turned their eyes toward the window which was beyond their eye level, prohibiting them from being able to see what was occurring outside. It was evident that the storm with its deadly quietness was still hovering over them, for the greenish grayness was still filtering through the bars of the window.

Even though they were safe inside the building, the feeling of doom remained with Amy. She felt as if the storm was keeping them there…but for what intent? A cold chill traveled through her body.

While Amy cradled the ill child in her arms, Matthew spread the blanket on the floor to lay her upon. As Amy laid the limp child upon the blanket, she dropped to the floor at Chrissie's side as she trembled with renewed fear. Her fear of the storm was replaced with a deep concern for Chrissie who was becoming sicker with every minute.

Beads of perspiration from the fever clung to Chrissie's forehead, and tendrils of her damp hair stuck to her flushed cheeks. Stroking Chrissie's fine blond hair, Amy felt helpless as she watched her drift off into a restless sleep.

Thrashing about in her fevered condition, Chrissie relinquished her hold on her doll by casting it aside to lie forgotten on the earthen floor.

Her eyes brimming over with tears, Amy appealed to Matthew for help in desperation. "I can't take this any longer. She is burning up with the fever. If we don't get help for her soon, she could die."

Matthew sitting on the floor next to Amy and Chrissie, felt vulnerable himself, as he cast his gaze toward the window again, and contemplated, searching for a solution. Abruptly, he rose to his feet, and started for the door.

"Matthew, where are you going?" Amy asked, panic mounting within her.

"This has gone far enough. This has to end," Matthew answered in a firm and final voice. "I'm going outside to see what is going on. Maybe it is safe enough now to go home. If so, we can get help for Chrissie. I have to go see. I'll be right back."

"No, Matthew, don't go. Oh, please don't leave us here alone," she begged in pure panic, her heart pounding, and her breath catching in her throat.

He didn't know how or what had to be done, but he couldn't stand helplessly by, not doing anything. He couldn't let his daughter die.

"I have to go. Maybe a passerby will come along. It's our only hope now. Wait here, I will find help. I'll be back as soon as I can," Matthew said hurriedly, as he gave her a quick kiss and headed for the door.

"Please don't go, Matthew. I don't want anything happening to you. I'm afraid of the storm, and with Chrissie so sick...Please don't leave us here alone. Please don't go."

Matthew was almost to the door despite Amy's pleading objections. She jumped to her feet to stop him, but he didn't get any farther.

With an enormous vehemence, the door burst open, knocking loose the large beam that was braced against it. The heavy beam came tottering down in full force. It all happened much too quickly for Matthew to react--or to escape.

"Matthew," Amy screamed. Horrified, she stood motionless, watching the beam topple onto Matthew, knocking him unconscious.

Starting to step forward to rush to his aid, she abruptly stopped, her face turning a ghastly white. Amy stood rooted, unable to move. She opened her mouth to scream, but no sound would come. She was paralyzed to the core.

The only feeling she had was of the rumbling and churning scream...roaring, boiling, starting ever so slowly in her toes, and working its way upward through her body to her throat, before finally erupting like a giant volcano. She screamed...and screamed again. Her screams echoed as they bounced against the walls. It wasn't until Amy collapsed to the floor into a deep darkness that the screams faded.

Chapter 13

They came. Through the open door, through the barred windows they came. They floated, they twisted and turned. They rose and dove. They hovered and drifted. They appeared and disappeared, only to appear again. They came like a multitude of ghosts--green ghosts--eerie, slimy, and spineless....

#

Amy fought from regaining consciousness. She welcomed the safety of oblivion. A nagging inner voice, however, was reminding Amy that her husband and child needed her, and it was forcing her to open her eyes. She prayed for all of this to be only a terrible dream.

Opening her eyes, she realized it was no dream. Thinking she must be insane, her mind raced. She knew this couldn't be real. It can't be happening. She is at home tending to Chrissie, and Matthew is feeding the cattle. With a slow-growing fear, Amy became more aware. Sounds were becoming eminent. A strange low eerie whooshing sound, separate and unfamiliar, was growing stronger and clearer, bringing her into full awareness.

As the room spun around her, she, unsteadily, rose with caution from the floor; however, the movement attracted the attention of the largest of the grotesque creatures.

The horrifying creature advanced toward her, flashing its fiery green tentacles at her. The appalling movement caused Amy to let out a piercing scream as she recoiled from the horrible being. Stumbling backwards, she tripped on the edge of Chrissie's blanket, and landed on the floor next to her. Instinctively, her arm reached toward Chrissie to protect her.

Seemingly satisfied that she had done as it had intended, the green monster withdrew a short distance from her, but continued hovering nearby keeping a watchful eye.

Too terrified to move, nor daring to, Amy sat immobile on the floor, trying to think rationally. With her eyes wide with fear, she focused on the creature's movements about the room. She wondered if this was only a figment of her imagination caused by her shock, or if things such as this horridness could actually occur. She thought that if she closed her eyes tightly, when she would open them, the terror would not have been.

She put her plan to the test, and she failed. Bewildered, Amy studied the bizarre phenomena before her eyes as the green slimy-looking apparitions continued carousing around the room. Their movements caused the flame in the lantern to flicker and threaten to go out, producing brief periods of darkness except for the greenish cast entering the room from the open door and window. The creatures would often whisk near Amy, causing her to recoil.

Peering at them, she tried to put a name to the eerie green monsters, but couldn't. They weren't human, nor were they animal, even though they had faces. Their mouths were narrow slits without lips, and their noses inconspicuous small protrusions in the center of their faces.

But their eyes--huge coal-black eyes--were the sole dominant feature that showed their souls. These mysterious beings didn't have to speak. Their eyes spoke for them.

Amy further observed that the horrifying creatures were of different sizes: tiny ones aimlessly floating about, and threatening larger ones that were hovering nearby. Most varied in size from three to five feet in height. They were much like ghosts--terrifying green ghosts.

Their horrifying green slimy bodies dissolved into wisps. Their arms were licks of green flames with spindly green tentacles forever reaching....

As Amy watched in terror, the floating green creatures began to drift back out through the open door and window. Did she dare to hope they were leaving? Watching their disappearance, she emitted a deep sigh of relief all too soon. Her breath caught in her throat when she realized she was mistaken.

She saw that not of all of them had gone, for five of the larger creatures had remained in the room. Keeping vigil over their captives, the creatures constantly floated and hovered about the room.

The largest of the group appeared to be the leader of the lot as it hovered nearest to Amy, forbidding her to move from her position. She had a startling impression that this thing was almost humanlike.

She shrank back with horror that this unbelievable creature could be capable of touching her, or even worse. The thought was revolting. She began to shake as the fearful images built in her mind. All she could do was cower near Chrissie and wait in fear of what would occur.

With her motherly instinct, she slowly backed inch by inch to position her body protectively between her child and the dangerous-looking apparitions that continued to hover about the room.

Restricted from going to the aid of her unconscious husband, Amy watched for any sign of movement from him. She could only wonder in terror if he was still alive.

She couldn't bear the thought of Matthew dying. She wouldn't know what to do without him. She refused to think it. He can't... he won't.

Shifting her gaze to Chrissie who was now sleeping more peacefully, Amy was thankful that Chrissie was unaware of what was happening, and didn't see these horrible monsters. It would have been too much for a small child to witness. Touching Chrissie's face, Amy was comforted when she saw that the fever had seemed to abate some. Her flesh felt cooler to the touch, and her face was no longer flushed.

"Amy..." Matthew said in a low murmur, as he began to regain consciousness. He raised his hand to feel the large lump on his forehead, caused by the wooden beam when it had fallen and stricken him.

Upon hearing Matthew groan, intense relief flooded through Amy that he was alive. Discarding all caution, she leaped to her feet to rush to his side, but she was stopped when the leader, anticipating her movement, blocked her way, while the other creatures approached nearer.

Amy held her breath in anticipation as she watched him slowly opening his eyes, but he was still too groggy to see anything clearly. He only saw huge green spots floating around him. He rubbed his glazed eyes, but in his mind's indistinctness, only the hazy green spots were visible to him.

"Matthew, thank goodness you are okay," Amy said, relieved that he was alive. "You are okay...aren't you? Oh no, you are bleeding. How bad are you hurt?" she asked anxiously, remembering the severe blow to his head. She wanted desperately to go to his side, but the sinister-looking phantoms hovering around her prohibited her from going to him.

"Yes...I think so...Am still rather dizzy. Everything seems blurry and...I'm seeing spots," Matthew answered in confusion, as he gingerly touched his wounded and bleeding forehead. He looked at his bloody fingers as he brought them away from the wound. Blood was trickling down the side of his brow and onto his cheek. "What happened?" Matthew asked. I can't remember...I think I must have hit my head on something."

His head roaring with strange low droning sounds, he attempted to brush away from his blurry eyes the greenish spots that seemed to continue swirling around him.

"The beam fell on you when you started to go for help," Amy answered from where she stood. "Are you sure you are all right? You are bleeding badly." Being concerned for his well-being, she momentarily forgot he was yet unaware of the bizarre danger they were now in.

Matthew tried to sit up, but he was unable to. He was still much too groggy. It entered his dazed mind that he must have suffered a mild concussion, as bits and pieces of what had happened began to come slowly together like a jigsaw puzzle.

A cloud...Amy's dream...trying to outrun the storm. The accident...- fleeing on foot. Amy falling...

Amy!

"Are you all right, Amy? I remember now, you had fallen. Is the baby--" Matthew didn't finish his question when he painstakingly turned his head toward the direction from where her voice had come. His eyes slowly came into focus. Sitting up, his eyes widening in disbelief, he became alert to the grotesque surroundings.

His heart stood still when he saw Amy standing helplessly in the middle of the dank room with terror written on her face. Hovering about her were the terrifying ghost-like apparitions. It was the most shocking and bizarre sight he could ever have imagined.

"My God! What is this?" he yelled, sweeping his widened eyes around him. "Am I hallucinating…or what? What is going on? Amy? Oh, my God…Amy."

"Be careful, Matthew. Oh, no."

Matthew's loud exclamation alerted the green ghastly creatures' attention, and they began coming at him from all directions. They soared all around him, whipping at him angrily. "What is going on here? Who…what are they?"

"I have no idea, but please be careful."

"Are you sure you are all right, and what about Chrissie? Did they hurt you in any way?"

"We're okay for now, but Matthew, please get us out of here. This is horrible. I can't stand much more of this. I'm so afraid."

With a strength developed from sheer fright, Matthew struggled to his feet. He flailed at the creatures with both arms, but it was to no avail. Where his fists struck each time, he hit nothing. His arms disappeared into a cloud of vacuum, leaving him defenseless. He could feel nothing of what the creatures were made; however, he continued to lash out at the horrible monsters even though his efforts proved to be ineffective.

Although it was verified that the beings couldn't be harmed, it was apparent that their tempers were riled. Their anger showed in their glaring black as they swarmed around Matthew. Twisting and turning, their serpent-like bodies skillfully dodged his flailing, but fortunately never touching him.

Desperate to reach Amy and Chrissie, Matthew calculated the risk he would have to take. Within a split second, he made a dash toward Amy, who in quick response ran into his arms.

The couple desperately clung together in the depths of despair and fear while the green creatures hovered around them, showing their enormous displeasure to have been thus outwitted. The leader, sending his talons pointedly between the man and woman, forced them apart. Clearly positioning himself between them, the creature advanced toward Amy.

Panic like she had never known before welled in her throat. A cold knot formed in her stomach.

Instantly, she understood the leader's unspoken intention, as he began to direct her toward the inner room. She had no choice but to obey and to precede him. She knew she had to try to stay calm; panicking wouldn't solve anything. Stumbling ahead of the creature's urging, she looked back over her shoulder toward Matthew, sending him a silent plea for help.

"Amy...no...Amy." Matthew, powerless to help her, could only stand in despair. A sensation of intense sickness and desolation swept over him, as he watched her disappear through the door and into the other room. The door closed, separating him from his wife, possibly forever.

Dropping to the floor at his daughter's side in utter dismay, he lowered his head to his up-drawn knees and wept.

Chapter 14

Upon entering the second room, Amy heard the creaking sound of the door slowly closing behind her. A flicker of apprehension and dread coursed through her, as she glanced back at the ominous green leader for instructions of what he wanted from her. In her fearful mind, she could only imagine what his intention could be.

Again, her panic overtook her, as the horrific green monster came nearer to her, apparently to urge her onward. She had no choice but to precede him into the room. Amy attempted to remain rational, but instead she began to shake uncontrollably, bile rising in her throat. She was helpless to herself, or those she loved, wondering what was to happen to them all. She had never been more petrified in her entire life.

Suddenly, she cried out as she doubled over with an intense searing pain. It was evident that something horribly wrong was happening with the baby. The pain was unbearable. Yet, more unbearable to Amy, was the fear that she could be having a miscarriage. She and Matthew had been ecstatic about this baby, and she couldn't stand the thought of losing this baby.

"Oh, please, God, not this," she cried out in anguish, scalding tears rolling down her pale cheeks. "I can't lose my baby. Please don't let my baby die." Amy's knees were about to buckle from under her, causing her to stagger. The room was spinning precariously around her. She used all her willpower to remain standing on her unsteady feet. She could not give in. She knew without a doubt that she had to remain in control of herself in order to survive.

Through her pain, she vaguely noticed that the terrifying apparition was watching her closely. She was terrified of what he had planned to do with her.

When he saw her attention once again on him, he pointed to the wooden bench as he advanced nearer to her, forcing her to move backwards. Shrinking from him, Amy backed away until she could not go farther. As the back of her knees hit the bench that was set against the wall, she lost her balance and fell backward onto the hard surface. Her captor hovered above her as if he was satisfied that she had obeyed him.

"Don't touch me. Please let me...us go. Don't hurt us. I don't know what you want of me...of us, but please don't hurt my babies," Amy said, not knowing whether he understood anything she was saying. Her mind swirled, as her fear-ridden eyes riveted on him while she watched and waited. She wondered if these were only empty words to the terrible creature that was alone in the room with her. Is it possible that this creature could hear, or understand? "Please give me a clue. What is it you want?"

Drawing threateningly nearer, the green monster continued to hover over Amy. The color draining from her face, she could only cower against the wall behind her.

"Matthew, help me," Amy screamed loudly, but it became apparent to her upon hearing only silence that he couldn't come to her aid. She began to weep. Yielding to the sobs that shook her, she pleaded again and again," Please help me, Matthew. Help me. I need you...."

Somewhere in her mind, however, flashed the thought that Matthew, himself, was in danger and in dire need of help, unable to come to her rescue. She was afraid that he could be hurt, or even worse--dead. She, also, feared for Chrissie, and how she was withstanding this

ordeal, and what will happen to her. She pleaded to God for His help.

As Amy recoiled on the bench, the leader advanced alarmingly nearer. His grotesque tentacles, extending toward here, were near enough to touch her. She shrank away from him as far as she could, but the wall restrained her. She opened her mouth to scream again, but nothing would come. She tried to close her eyes against him and what would be, but she could not. She could only stare back into those huge black liquid eyes--and wait.

The pain in her womb being unbearable, and the terrible sense that she was going to die assailed her. She couldn't bear the agony any longer; the turmoil was much too great. Would she die from the pain or from the terrifying green creature that continued to hover over her? She didn't know which was worse…losing her baby, or dying in this horrendous way. There was the horrible thought of this sickening creature even raping her. Will it be before or after? She would rather die first.

Thoughts of the baby in her womb surfaced. She though of what the loss of the baby would do to her if she should survive, and to Matthew. Matthew was ecstatic when she had told him that they were going to have another baby. He hoped it would be a boy this time, a boy that would follow him around while he worked. He had such big plans to teach his son all about farming.

He talked endlessly about teaching his son how to drive the tractor and how to feed the cattle. Maybe in time, he would buy him a horse to ride. Now, it would never be.

Lying paralyzed without hope on the hard wooden bench, all Amy could do was to stare at the appalling creature lean nearer toward her, and wait for the inevitable to come. The thought of what he could, or would, do to her was past enduring to Amy. His revolting touch upon her body would be unbearable. Not being able to sustain any more agony, her mind began to recoil and drift from the horror of the present to the past.

Time stood still as months of memories came rushing back to her. Sad memories of the suffering she had endured. The hurt from her husband's neglect to her and their daughter…Her loneliness…Her terrible sense of rejection. Then, there were the remembrances of her cherished days and moments. Falling in love and marrying Matthew…the joy they felt when their daughter was born…leaving New York City to make a new life in rural Kansas with the promise that their marriage would be saved…their happiness, hopes, and dreams.

Everything she had ever felt tumbled all around her, a whirlwind of emotions in the green eerie dimness that filled the gloomy room. She thought of her precious Chrissie, too young to understand what was happening. She wondered if Chrissie would remember her. She will be without a mother to care for her, to administer to her needs.

"She needs me," Amy murmured. Amy thought of her and Matthew's love for each other, and the happiness they had shared together. They have had their problems like any other couple, but because of their strong enduring love, they had been able to resolve any problem that had come their way. She remembered his strong loving arms when he held her tenderly, whether they were happy and content, or when he comforted her. The last few months after coming to Kansas proved their marriage was becoming solid once again.

Slowly the past fell away, voices long since stilled, faces long forgotten; all were suddenly there with her, echoes and images of the past jostling for prominence among the terror at the presence. She needed Matthew's arms about her now. She wanted to tell him that she loved him with all her heart, and wanted him to be happy, not sad. Goodbye my love, my darling. I love you.... She regretted that she could not tell Chrissie goodbye. Forgive me, my beautiful and precious daughter. I love you....

"Oh, God, help me. Let me die now. I don't want to know any more, nor do I want to feel. Please..." she cried out, before her words faded into a suffocated moan. Her head bowed, her body slumping in despair, she waited for her inevitable death. She had reached the end.

The slimy sinister-looking creature was almost upon her, his head and wispy tentacles drawing nearer, almost to the point of making physical contact with her. She could feel his breath upon her face.

A long, silent scream echoed through her brain. From somewhere deep within, she found the strength for one last desperate plea, as she lifted her gaze to the hovering creature.

"Please don't harm my family...and me," she managed to say in a weak and tremulous voice that rose to a piercing tone before dying into silence, "Please...NOooooooo." Unable to block away her destiny, she closed her eyes tightly for she couldn't endure any more.

"A.. my."

Amy heard the voice that seemed to come from a long way off. Was it Matthew calling her, or was it Chrissie, awake and needing her? In her dazed mind, she could not tell. At the sound of the voice, she lifted her head and listened. She managed to force her eyes open, blinked, and focused her gaze. All she could see was the terrifying green creature that still loomed over her.

"A..my."

Again, the voice spoke out to her. It took her a moment to realize that the childlike sound she heard came from within the creature that was hovering over her. His dark eyes were studying her with a concerned intensity. Half-rising, her mouth dropped open in disbelief as she stared at the captor who had spoken her name.

"You...you can...speak?" Amy asked, the shock causing the words to wedge in her throat. Icy fear twisted in her heart, as chilling thoughts raced through her mind. *If this monster is able to speak, what else is he capable of doing?* "Who are you? What do you want?" she asked, a faint thread of hysteria trembled in her voice. "Tell me why you are keeping us prisoners here."

He didn't answer her questions. He regarded her quizzically for a time, watching her with his huge black eyes. Feeling drawn into the endless dark depth of those eyes, she could only stare back at him.

Terrified of what was taking place, she was only dimly aware of the bright flash of light that lit the dim room for a moment, and the clap and roar of the tremendous thunder that shook the walls and the bench beneath her. A random thought entered her mind. *It's going to rain after all. The fields needed it. Matthew will be pleased.*

Amy held her breath when the green being's tentacle slowly reached out to her--a green wisp flicking toward her body. She could not speak. Panting in terror, she gasped as she recoiled from him. What she had feared the most was undoubtedly about to happen. Suddenly her heart stood still; she was unable to move. She wondered if she had dreamed it, or whether it actually happened.

Yet, the horrible creature was there--she saw him with her

own eyes. It was all too real; there was no denying it. It did happen.

A thin green wisp of the flicking flame touched her...where her baby lay inside her. Although she was aware he had touched her, Amy did not feel the physical contact, other than experiencing an unexplainable sensation which was inconceivable.

Almost at the point of touching her again, he pointed to Amy's belly, and in an odd gentle tone, said softly, "Ba..by. Ba.. by okay." His gaze, soft as a caress, radiated with an aura of tenderness as he looked deep into her fear-stricken eyes.

Upon his gentle touch, Amy immediately sensed with a pulse-pounding certainty that her baby was alive and well. She knew at that moment that both her life, as well as her baby's, would be spared. As if she was under a hypnotic spell, Amy became calm and comforted in that knowledge.

Amy came to the realization that these creatures weren't going to harm them. Whatever reason he or they were keeping them there must be for their protection. There couldn't be any other explanation.

Continuing his vigil beside her, the green creature didn't attempt to touch her further, and Amy began to relax somewhat, her breathing settling to an even rhythm. She gazed into the deep pools of his black eyes and saw genuine concern for her, and for her baby.

She was overwhelmed by the new turn of events. She had the distinct feeling that there was no longer an immediate need to be frightened of her captor. Even the intense pain inside her was gradually subsiding. Even though the circumstances had dramatically changed, Amy was aware she must still remain cautious. She wasn't about to take any chances of provoking these mystifying and unpredictable creatures, not knowing what would happen if they would become agitated again.

There were still too many unanswered questions in her mind concerning these strange creatures, as a tumble of confused thoughts and feelings assailed her. Who are these creatures? Where did they come from?

The storm.

She wondered if it was possible these beings were somehow associated with the storm.

The same eerie green...

The warning...

Had the warning been about the storm, or of these creatures...or could it have been both? She asked herself if there was yet to be something else of which she was not aware. Something so terrible she could not remember...or her mind willing to accept.

Slowly Amy struggled to sit up from where she was lying on the bench and swung her legs over the side. Testing her strength, she found that even though she was unsteady on her feet she was able to stand. Her pain subsiding, she was now positive that the baby in her womb was going to be all right.

Keeping a watchful eye on her captor, she, however, was aware she would have to guard her own actions, as well as his. No one could predict what more they would do. Carefully, she moved unsteadily toward the door that led to the outer room where her husband and child were confronting their own personal torments.

Chapter 15

Grieving with sorrow, Matthew sat in silence by his daughter's side. His tears had subsided; his sense of loss was beyond tears. He was at a total loss as how he was to going to rescue his wife and daughter from the terrorizing predicament they were in.

Gazing upon the small child as she slept peacefully, he absent-mindedly fingered the soft fabric of her pink rompers. Thinking how precious she was to him and Amy, he was thankful that she was completely unaware of the horror surrounding them. Yet, he was devastated that there was nothing he could do to safeguard her safety.

Shifting his gaze toward the door of the inner room where the ominous leader was holding Amy captive, Matthew worried about what was occurring in there, whether she was alive...or dead. He immediately reprimanded himself for even thinking it. He had to believe that Amy was all right. She had to be. Life would be meaningless without her.

He listened with a keen ear for any sound he could hear. At one point, he thought he heard her cry out. Acting instinctively upon hearing the sound, Matthew leaped to his feet and took a few steps toward the door. Before he could reach the door, however, the threatening horde hovering around him barricaded his way. It was apparent the creatures weren't going to let him pass to go to Amy.

Matthew desperately needed to find a way to help Amy some way. Not able to come up with a workable solution, he felt defeated. Shoving his hands in his pockets, his shoulders hunched forward as grief and despair overtook him. After a few moments, he lifted his head in determination and defiance, deciding it was his responsibility to save his family, and he would have to do whatever he must do.

Looking around the prison walls for a clue as how to save them, his eyes traveled to the entrance door. The green eerie glow of the mysterious storm continued to elongate through the open door and the barred window.

Gazing at the open door, Matthew had the idea that maybe there could be a way he could reach it to make his escape to go for the help they desperately needed. He thought that with some luck, someone, supposedly one of their neighbors, would come along that he could flag down to help them.

Shaking his head, Matthew decided to abandon the idea. Even if he could escape these monsters and go for help, he couldn't leave Amy and Chrissie here alone with them to suffer the consequences. He had to come up with another way.

Glancing at Chrissie, it became obvious he couldn't leave her side. He couldn't risk anything happening to her. On the other hand, Amy needed him, also. He asked himself how he was going to be able to get to her and, more importantly, how he was going to save her and Chrissie.

At the same time Matthew was contemplating about escaping, he thought he heard sounds coming from the next room. Listening attentively for Amy's voice, he was stunned when he realized that the voices he heard were more than one.

He was equally stunned when he heard Amy speaking to someone. He was puzzled of whom she was speaking with, for he wasn't aware of anyone coming into the building, except for the super beings, and they didn't talk.

"Amy, can you hear me? Please answer me if you can hear me," he called out, straining his ears for her reply. But none came. "Dammit, let me go to her. She needs me. I must go to her," Matthew cried out at the phantoms that were prohibiting him from going to her. They only glared back at Matthew, threatening him with their fiery black eyes.

Matthew decided he had to take the risk of trying to reach her where she was being kept captive. Slowly, he advanced toward the door, but the ominous green creatures prohibited his progress from coming nearer. Cautiously, Matthew maneuvered sideways, hoping to outmaneuver the captors; however, they were much too swift for him. Blocking his way, they prevented him from successfully sidestepping them.

Desperate to get to Amy, he frantically struck out at one of the nearby apparitions. The strike was useless. The unsuccessful attempt only infuriated the captor more, causing him to go into a violent rage, as he attacked Matthew.

Sudden flicks of strong electrical currents from the angry creature's green tentacles sent a forceful surge of energy bolting through the air toward his victim, followed by an extremely explosive tremor that shook the walls and floors of the building.

Unfortunately, Matthew had no time to escape the violent attack as the shockwave surged through his body, knocking him into a stupor as he fell to the floor.

Several minutes passed as he lay immobile. It became deadly quiet, the only sound coming from the low swishing from the floating phantoms, as they continued their angry carousing about the room. After some time passed, Matthew began to recover from the shock, as he gradually regained feelings in his body and mind. Searing, hot sensations surged throughout his head and limbs.

He felt the excruciating pain from every nerve ending in his body from the top of his head down to his toes. His entire body within felt as if it was afire. All the nerves in his body were affected, burning and crawling beneath his skin.

A tremendous weakness washed throughout him when he tried to sit up. He forced himself to rise upon his knees, but he could do no more. His spent body wasn't capable of obeying his mind's command. All he could do was shield himself with an uplifted arm as the angered horde threatened to strike again.

Eventually gaining some strength, Matthew, through determination and perseverance, managed to crawl back to Chrissie's side. Intending to protect her with his life, he positioned his body in front of her. He knew these creatures were dangerous and that they were capable of doing anything. He vowed that he would not allow these monsters to harm his daughter as long as there is an ounce of strength in his body. They would have to kill him first.

Slowly his body was returning to normalcy, although he was still trembling with weakness. With dazed eyes, he watched the evil phantoms with the perception that these creatures were very dangerous, and that he must be extremely careful not to provoke them further.

He ran his hand over his face as he contemplated about the dreadful creatures that were keeping him and his family prisoners. It occurred to him that they must have come with the storm, but how and--why?

Amy's premonition!

Besieged with annoyance at himself for not believing Amy when she tried to tell him about the warning she had, he blamed himself for the danger they were now in. He had shrugged off her pleadings, not believing her despite what she said. He thought it had only been a bad dream.

Remorsefully, he thought now that if he hadn't been such a fool, he would had believed and trusted her, and they would have left sooner--They could have escaped, and they would be safe now. The realization twisted and turned in his mind, as he looked for answers.

He had heard and read about extraterrestrial beings, however, he wasn't totally convinced that they actually did exist. Continuing to observe them, he decided that they weren't celestial beings, nor were they human. These being were more like ghosts-- green ghosts. These creatures didn't resemble anything that he had ever seen in print. Most books and literatures he had seen pictured
humanlike skeletal bodies with arms and legs like mankind.

The beings hovering around him were totally different. They remained aloft, never touching the floor. Their bodies were amorphous much like ghosts, except these were slimy lime green in coloring. The aura they emitted made it evident that these creatures were dangerous.

Matthew continued to deliberate as he kept his eyes on them for any clue that they might give. He wondered why these monsters, whatever they are, were keeping them here.

The volatile creatures had proven they were enormously evil and dangerous. Yet at times, it seemed they were just waiting, biding for time. But, for what? Whatever reason it could be was beyond Matthew's wildest expectation.

Shaking his head in frustration, there was no doubt in his mind that these supernatural beings were indestructible, and that he and his family would have to be extremely careful.

With the exception of their leader, the green apparitions continued their flitting all around the room. For the moment, it appeared that whenever their prisoner was passive, they would dart and frolic about, as if they were playing a game of tag with one another.

Because his decision had obviously been made for him, Matthew could only wait and watch--and pray. He, also, had plenty of time to think. Matthew buried his head in his hands in defeat. This time, however, he remained dry-eyed. There was too much to think about. Time stood still for him. He had time enough to reflect on his life, what had been, and what could have been.

He wished with all his heart they could go back in time, so he could have a second chance to do right by his family. He thought of how stupid he had been back in New York, and how he had thought only of his unhappiness and his own selfish dreams. Until now, he hadn't considered what it was doing to Amy, and how unfair he had been to her. Infuriatingly angry with himself, he balled his fists in disgust thinking that his selfishness has resulted in now putting them all in this horrible situation. How could he have been that blind?

"Please forgive me, Amy," he spoke aloud in the room where he and their daughter had been separated from his wife. "If anything happens to you or the babies, I could never forgive myself. Please, God, keep them safe. That is all I ask."

Unable to cease his self-blame, he thought of the many "If's". If...he hadn't kept dreaming of living on a farm. If...he hadn't brought his wife and daughter out to the middle of nowhere to fulfill his dreams, they would now be safe. If...he had believed Amy's warning, they would have had time to escape the storm. They would not have been held as prisoners in this in this God-forsaken place where they had taken refuge, and their lives would not have been endangered.

I wish we had never come here.

Amy's words from earlier that afternoon pounded in his head. His eyes showed the tortured dullness of disbelief and realization before he was overcome with different emotions, especially with guilt. He hadn't known that was how she felt, and he was flabbergasted. He had been positive she loved it here. She had said she did.

Forlornly, he prayed that it was not too late for him to tell her he was sorry.

Frustrated, weary…and angry…Matthew sat gazing about him as he searched for a way to get him and his family safely out of this horrible nightmare that seemed to never end.

Chapter 16

Lizzie Thornton worked diligently, constantly stirring the hot, thickening concoction in the heavy black iron kettle, waiting for it to come to a boil. She was doing what she liked best... preparing her herbs and spices to that she would later take into the Farmer's Market in Spring Hill.

With the heat generating from the hot stove where she was working, her kitchen was stifling with only the open window for cooling. Air-conditioning in her small home was a luxury that she didn't have.

With her free hand, Lizzie swiped at the moisture on her face. Streams of perspiration trickled down the creases of her furrowed face and continued down her wrinkled neck. One droplet on her forehead escaped her swipe and slowly trickled down the length of her nose.

Exasperated from the heat, Lizzie decided it was definitely time for her to take a well-deserved reprieve from toiling over the hot stove. Turning off the burner underneath the iron kettle, she hurriedly stepped outdoors to the front porch of her small house for some cooling air. Standing near the porch railing, she lifted her damp, hot face to the cooling breeze and inhaled the refreshing air. Scanning the late afternoon sky, she noticed a few scattered clouds drifting across the horizon. She, however, knew from experience that this kind of clouds wouldn't offer any rain.

After a while when feeling refreshed, Lizzie was about to return to her kitchen when she noticed the McCormacks speed past her lane in their small red vehicle, stirring up puffs of dust behind them. Frowning, she shook her head in disapproval with the speed of which they were traveling, thinking that they didn't realize such recklessness could be catastrophic. She watched until the dust began to settle before going back indoors to finish brewing her tonic.

As she was adding the assortment of herbs to the simmering kettle, Lizzie discovered she was running short of pokeweed. Remembering that she had seen some of the herb growing wild along the roadside, she turned off the burner under the kettle and snatched up a wicker basket.

Hurrying out the door, Lizzie said aloud to herself, "Also, some elderberry would be nice. I'll need some before long. I've seen some growing just down the road. I have to hurry though; the sun will be setting soon."

Lizzie's European-born mother had passed on the secrets that she had acquired from generations past of the various ways of using herbs and taught her how to prepare them. Lizzie continued making her mother's sworn-by tonics and potions, along with herbal teas of various kinds, believing wholeheartedly in their tried and true effectiveness.

She enjoyed searching and gathering the wild herbal leaves and berries to use in many different ways, besides growing many kinds of herbs in her garden. In essence, her herbal garden took precedence over all else when it came to neatness, often neglecting her household duties.

After gathering the valued herbs, she would hang the herbs and berries in upside down bunches from the ceiling where they would be left to dry until needed. Scattered about in her cluttered kitchen were an assortment of wicker baskets heaped with herbs and roots.

Lizzie spent many hours filling the bottles and jars with the prepared herbs, whether they were to be dried and crushed, or made into tonics and ointments. She labeled the finished products with pride before she would carry them the five miles to the market. She would return at the day's end with income to sustain herself a while longer in her modest way of living.

Hurrying down the lane to the main road with renewed energy, Lizzie turned northward, keenly searching the roadside for the desired herbs, gathering up whatever wild herbs she happened upon. She was pleased to find an abundant supply of various herbs that were available during the early summer season.

A short distance down the road, Lizzie looked up from her searching, and paused when she noticed something red up ahead.

With her eyesight not being as good as it once had been, she had to squint to bring the red object into focus.

"Oh, my God. It isn't...Oh please, don't let it be them," she said aloud. Fearing that it was indeed what she anticipated, she quickened her pace. As Lizzie drew nearer, she gasped when she saw that her presumption was correct. She recognized the red convertible that belonged to the McCormack family.

"No, it can't be. No, not them," Lizzie cried out, dropping her wicker basket, causing the contents to spill out upon the ground. In anguish, she brought her trembling liver-spotted hands up to her timeworn face. She moaned aloud, her memories of the past surfacing to crowd out the present.

The scene brutally reminded Lizzie of the other accident that had occurred many years ago, which had taken the lives of her beloved Phillip and sweet little Elizabeth, her only child.

"No, this can't be happening again--not again," Lizzie cried aloud, as flashbacks of the former accident became more vivid in her memory. The horrible visions of the past intermingled with the scene that lay before her, visions she had tried hard not to think about, and to accept. It had been much too unbearable.

Collapsing to her knees in the middle of the deserted road, she yielded to the compulsive sobs that shook her. She tried not to remember that awful tragedy, but the memories came rushing forth.

Moaning in agony, she began to mutter incoherently, "Phillip, no. No, not Phillip. Elizabeth, my baby...my sweet little girl. Open your eyes. I've got to wash that blood off. Phillip, get up. I see something red. What is that red? My baby...my little girl...my beautiful Elizabeth. I have your doll here for you. She is not moving. Why isn't she moving? She's as white as a sheet. Wake up, Elizabeth. Why isn't she waking up? No, she can't be...NOoooooo."

Tormented, the hysterical woman continued her chaotic behavior, rocking back and forth, writhing in anguish as she mourned at last after the forty long years of suppressing her grief. Weeping loudly, she swayed her slight body back and forth as she gave vent to the agony of her loss. She ran her bony fingers through her unruly hair, yanking handfuls from her scalp, not ever feeling the pain. Her hurt of years ago was much too great.

Lizzie could see the event unfold as if it had just occurred. She fought the images that were surfacing, but she lost the battle.

She remembered the two uniformed officers from the Spring Hill police department at her door, the whirling lights on the police cars flashing brightly, the sympathy in their eyes when they came to break the news to her.

She remembered the intersection where the accident had occurred, the ambulance crew already on the scene when she had gotten there.

She remembered the drunken driver. He had escaped with his life.

She remembered the horrible wreckage. The blood--so much blood. It was everywhere.

She remembered the twisted and broken body of her husband, Phillip--dead--and her precious little girl in the hospital lying in a deep coma like a broken doll, never to awaken.

Lizzie remembered it all.

Several long minutes passed before the crazed woman, weakened from her emotional outburst, began to recover her sanity. Slowly straightening her trembling body, she looked through her blurred eyes toward the red vehicle that had brought back all the vivid details of the tragic accident that had happened many years ago.

Her legs trembling unsteadily, Lizzie awkwardly rose to her feet. She bit her lips in concentration as she twisted her rheumatic hands together. Her mind returning to the present, the long-ago tragedy was hazily being replaced with a red vehicle on the roadside teetering dangerously over the edge of the deep embankment.

"Oh my, what am I going to do? I have to get help for them. They could be trapped inside. Please, Lord, don't let that little girl...I hope she isn't in that car. Please, it can't happen again--not again. I can't let it. I have to do something," Lizzie said aloud, imposing an iron control on herself. A sense of strength overcame her and her earlier despair lessened.

She hitched up her long burdensome skirt, and began rushing homeward to phone for help, the coarse gravel under her feet hindering her awkward haste. Her wicker basket was left abandoned where she had dropped it, her precious herbs strewn onto the ground.

Lizzie was only a few feet from the lane leading toward her small house when a large roar caused her to look upward to see a giant ball of blinding light falling from the sky, seemingly right in front of her. Following was a huge thundering explosion that shook the ground underneath her feet. The intense tremor knocked Lizzie forcefully to the ground.

"Merciful Heavens, the world is coming to an end," Lizzie cried out in horror as she lay face down in the gravel, too terrified to move, or to feel the pain from the bloodied abrasions on her hands and knees.

The ground shook while a great thundering rumble roared Lizzie could not move. She lay immobile, too frightened to move, until gradually the shaking ground underneath her had subsided, and the loud roar had quieted. After several moments had passed without any further occurrences, Lizzie cautiously raised her head and looked around. Rising painstakingly upon her hands and knees, she saw a huge orange glow filtering through the trees.

"I have to get home...I have to get help," Lizzie said aloud, frantically gathering her skirt about her to enable her to run more quickly. "Lord, give me the strength. I have to get help for these people. Who do I call? I know. I will call Harry. He'll know what to do."

With a strength found from sheer necessity, the old woman ran as quickly as her age would allow. She was unmindful of the pain from her bleeding hands and legs. There were much more important things to think about other than a few minor scrapes and bruises.

Lizzie was almost within reach of her home, but she felt as if it was yet a mile away. Panting laboriously with fatigue, she didn't know if she could make the final steps to her door. However, she was determined that she had to try as long as there was an ounce of strength left in her body. With that determination, she didn't slow her pace.

As Lizzie reached the front porch of her house, she tripped on a wooden step, knocking the wind out of her, but still nothing could slow her down. She pulled herself up to her hands and knees, and crawled up the remaining two steps, then struggled to stand on her wobbling legs.

At last, she was at the door, but before she stepped inside, she hesitantly glanced with apprehension toward the McCormack's property. It was beyond her what was possibly taking place at her neighbors. But for the moment, she didn't have time to think about what was occurring. She had to get help for her young neighbors as soon as possible first.

Lizzie dashed to the telephone, and then paused. She couldn't remember Harry's number. Running a hand across her face in dismay, she tried to think. After a few harrowing minutes passed, she remembered the business card that Harry had at one time given her with his telephone number on it. He had given it to her in the event she should ever need to reach him... just in case she should need him. She needed him now.

She hurried to the antique roll-top desk and rummaged nervously through several compartments, scattering papers about until she finally found the small, age-yellowed card bearing Harry's telephone number.

Sighing with relief that she had been able to find the card, Lizzie hurried back with it to the telephone, and dialed. In utter dismay, she heard the telephone ringing and ringing, time after time.

"Please, Harry, be there. Please answer the phone. You have to answer--I need you."

Unfortunately, Harry did not answer. He wasn't there to answer her desperate plea for help.

Chapter 17

Matthew sat on the floor near Chrissie, shielding her body from the hovering beings. Totally engrossed in his thoughts, he didn't see, nor hear Amy enter the room until she spoke.

"Matthew..."

Wheeling toward the direction from where her soft voice came, his face brightened with relief to hear her speak his name. He met her gaze as she stood in the doorway with a beginning of a smile tipping the corners of her mouth. His gaze traveled over her face and searched her eyes. Elated to see her, he thought that she had never looked more like an angel than at that moment. A muscle quivered at his jaw as he reverently prayed that this was not an illusion.

Amy began to move toward him, but Matthew, fearful of what the hovering horde of phantoms would do, held up his hand in gesture for her to stop from coming farther. He didn't intend to take any chances that might provoke their captors and put them all in further danger.

"Wait, Amy, don't move. These creatures are dangerous. We must be careful."

Disregarding his warning, she rushed to him. Dropping to the floor, she threw herself into his arms.

"It's okay. They won't harm us," Amy answered, assuredly. "Matt, we are safe."

"What do you mean? How can you say these evil monsters won't hurt us?" Matthew asked in bewilderment and bitterness as he searched her face. "They have already done quite enough to endanger our lives, and who knows what else they will do. Don't expect me to trust these horrible beings."

"Yes, Darling, I know. I don't understand it, but I feel they are keeping us here for some reason other than to harm us. Maybe they are here to protect us from something," Amy answered softly, as she thought of the possibility, regardless of how bizarre it seemed.

"Amy, have you lost your mind? Whatever do you mean?" he asked. He bit his lips together to prevent saying more, when he remembered once before he had made the serious mistake of not believing her.

She gestured toward the docile throng floating about, as she replied, "Look for yourself, Matt, they're leaving us alone. They aren't paying any attention to us. We are safe. We only need to be cautious in not provoking them."

Looking about, Matthew had to agree for the time being that she was correct in her assumption, and he began to calm down. Gathering her into his arms, he held her snugly, never wanting to let go. Sinking into his cushioning embrace, and with a sigh of pleasure, she relaxed against him. He had no idea what would occur next, or if they would ever get out of this dreadful place alive. Nevertheless, he was thankful to finally be able to once again hold his wife in his arms.

"Look, Matt," Amy whispered, interrupting Matthew's thoughts, as she nodded with a tilt of her head toward where Chrissie was sleeping.

Matthew immediately turned his gaze to where Amy, her mouth curled into a smile, was watching in fascination. They were both amazed by what they were witnessing.

The smallest of the creatures had picked up Chrissie's doll that she had forgotten on the floor where she had previously dropped it. With the rag doll in his grasp, he floated over to the sleeping child. Gentleness emitted from his dark eyes, as he placed the doll into the curve of her outstretched arm and lightly brushed his tentacle across her cheek.

Though Chrissie was sound asleep, she instinctively clutched the doll to her, while the empathetic young creature hovered over her with a compassionate gaze.

Smiling, Amy felt a warm glow envelope her and she gloried in the shared moment, as she and Matthew watched in amazement.

"Why...I'll be damned," Matthew said, his eyes widening in astonishment as he watched in wonder. He thought that if these creatures had feelings of compassion, then they could possibly be human after all. It flashed through his mind the old adage about wonders never seeming to cease, and knew it was true.

Emotionally touched by the creature's gentle action, Amy and Matthew were both somewhat fearful and bewildered, for they still had no answers of the being's identity. They only knew that they were safe--for the time being.

Amy and Matthew, still immobilized in the creature's power, kept close vigil over their captors, who continued to float and carouse about. The green creatures, at the present time, didn't appear to be much threat to the imprisoned family, so Amy and Matthew were able to finally let their guard down somewhat.

"Amy, Darling, I am truly sorry."

"Whatever for?"

"Wait, don't say anything. Please let me finish because I have much to say to you...something I should have said long before."

"Matthew, what is it? You sound so serious."

He gazed into her questioning eyes, conveying the importance of what he was about to say. "I didn't realize until now that it could have been too late," he continued. "I could have lost you, and I wouldn't have been able to tell you. Nor could I have stood losing you and Chrissie...and the baby. You and the babies are my life."

"All right, Matthew, I am listening. But, why is it so important that you have to tell me right now?"

"Please hear me out, Amy."

"Okay, I'm here...tell me."

Tears ran down Matthew's face while he spoke hurriedly, afraid to slow down. It had to be said--and it had to be said now. "I am totally to blame," Matthew said apologetically. "I should have listened to you sooner. If I had, we could have escaped the storm, and we would have all been safe. If I had only listened to you and believed in your instinct, we wouldn't have been trapped here in this God-forsaken place."

Amy started to protest, but Matthew silenced her lips with his fingertips, "No, Amy, please let me finish. There is more. I need and want to say this."

With desperation showing in his grave face, he continued in a rush of words. "It is entirely my fault. I know now that I was wrong. I shouldn't have brought you and Chrissie here to Kansas. I have been unfair to you."

Amy started to protest, but he wouldn't let her. Before she could say anything, Matthew rushed on. "I was wrapped up in my own selfish dreams and self-pity. I forgot that they were my dreams--not yours, not ours--but my own. Can you ever forgive me?"

Amy wanted to stop his flow of words, but she remained silent. She didn't want him to continue blaming himself, except she knew that he needed to say the words, whether they were true or not.

With his eyes wide with a fearful acknowledgment, Matthew continued, "Because of my selfishness, I could have lost you, Chrissie and the baby."

With tears of compassion in her eyes, she shook her head, protesting, "No, don't. Oh, no...Darling, don't say that. You are wrong. You weren't--"

Interrupting her, Matthew was persistent on having his say. "I love you, Amy. I wouldn't be able to live if I had lost you. You are my life, my everything."

"I love you too, more than life itself. But, Matt, what happened today was not your fault."

"I promise you, if we get out of this safely, we will go back to New York City. I should never have brought you and Chrissie here. It was a foolish mistake, and all because of my own selfish dreams."

"Stop it, Matthew. You have to listen to me. Stop berating yourself like this."

"But it was my fault. I am totally to blame, all because of my dreams about having a farm here in Kansas once again."

"It wasn't only your dream--It became mine, also. Matt, I wanted it just as much as you did. Besides, don't you know I would go to the end of the world just to be with you? Don't you see how happy we have been since we have moved to Kansas?"

"But you said, Amy...you said earlier you wished we hadn't come here."

"Oh my gosh, Matt. I'm so sorry. I didn't mean it. Please forgive me. I was overwrought with fear at the time, and I didn't realize what I was saying. I never intended to hurt you, please trust me. I didn't mean it."

"Are you saying you aren't sorry that we came here? Do you not want to go back to New York?"

Breaking into a broad and joyous smile, Amy threw herself into his arms, and answered, "New York? No, Silly. I never want to go back there. I love it here. This is our home now, and we will stay here forever. This is where our children will grow up and where their children will always have a place to come."

Putting her away from him, Matthew searched her face looking for assurance that she was honestly being sincere with what she was saying. "I'm relieved to hear you say that, Amy. I was afraid you weren't happy here, and you wanted to go back to New York. All I want is for you to be happy. Are you absolutely certain you want to stay here? We will go back if you--"

"Do you hear me, Matt? I love it here...I don't even mind Lizzie Thornton and her bizarre ways. At least she adds a little spice to our lives," Amy said, giggling at the pun she made regarding the old woman recluse and her herbs.

Matthew stepped toward her once again and clasped her body close to his. His lips swooped down to meet hers.

Feeling giddy with their renewed happiness, they forgot for a moment where they were until a whoosh of air brought them back to reality.

A bevy of the green apparitions of assorted sizes was returning--floating, drifting--as they filled the room. They darted and chased. They teased and hovered. The creatures were everywhere. The whooshing motion of the beings caused the flame in the lantern to flicker, about to be extinguished.

Matthew and Amy leaped to their feet in astonishment and clung tightly to one another, fear griping them once more. Regardless of what was to happen, they did not intend to lose physical contact with each other again.

"What the hell?" Matthew blurted out in bewilderment, as the green ghosts cascaded and caroused about the room. "Will this never end?"

Suddenly pointing to the entrance door, Amy said in amazement as she stared at the phenomena, "Matthew, look. They are leaving...They are actually leaving. It is incredible."

Matthew's heart quickened as they stared--for it was true. The eerie green creatures were leaving. A few reappeared, and then disappeared. It was apparent that a greater number of the green apparitions were leaving the way they came. They were leaving--fading away.

However, as the horde diminished from the room, their leader returned, floating about. Amy and Matthew held their breaths in anticipation of what he would do next. Unable to move, they stood watching in silence. The green creature circled around the room, looking from one to the other, before he headed back to the open door.

When he reached the door, he paused and turned to face Matthew and Amy, his gaze lingering briefly on Amy. With a small nod of his head, and with the slightest hint of a smile on his lipless mouth, the green leader of the horde turned and disappeared through the open door, vanishing as if he had never been.

The whooshing sound of the throng's presence was gone. A quiet descended upon the now empty room.

With disbelief and wonder, the couple clung together in silence to absorb what they are just witnessed. They stood there, blank, amazed, and much shaken.

"Did they..."

"Do you think..."

A tense silence enveloped the room while they stared at the open door. Amy's breath catching in her throat, she asked in a low voice, "Do you think they have really gone for good?"

"I think so," Matthew answered, flabbergasted. "You know...I do believe they have."

Releasing Amy from his arms, Matthew hurried to slam shut

the heavy door in hope of preventing the green creatures' return. He refused to think that they could return and gain entrance again.

It didn't occur to Matthew, however, to check on the condition of the storm which had driven him and his family to the shelter of this building before he shut the door. His only thought was on the horde of the mysterious green creatures that had kept them in a terrorizing prison.

Once he was assured they were safe, Matthew took Amy into his arms. He lowered his head against Amy's shoulder as she buried her face against his chest. He felt a deep sigh emitting between their bodies. He wasn't sure whether it had come from her, or from him. He raised his head and looked toward the window where he could faintly hear the gentle breeze filtering through the bars. He marveled at the thought that it sounded like music to his ears.

"Look, Amy. A star," Matthew exclaimed as he looked upward toward the barred window. Seeing the clear evening sky brought him renewed hope. "The stars are out, which means the storm has passed."

Amy looked up, following Matthew's gaze toward the window. Filled with a joyous relief, she saw the first stars of the evening twinkling brightly. More importantly, the glow of the eerie green color had vanished.

The late evening sounds of the countryside were delightfully apparent. Amy marveled at the wonderful sound which previously had been annoying to her. The sound of chirping crickets was now a blessing to her ears.

Within moments, Chrissie stirred as she awakened from her long and deep sleep. She had forgotten her whereabouts and wailed frightfully as she sat up, "Mommy? Daddy? Where are you?"

Overcome with relief that everything was returning to normalcy, Amy rushed to gather the child into her arms while Matthew went to survey the situation outside.

"We are right here, Chrissie. There is nothing to be afraid of,

Sweetie. Everything is okay," Amy assured the child and herself, as she caressed Chrissie's face.

She was relieved to find that the child's fever had broken. Although she was enormously comforted, Amy was mystified when the thought entered her mind that the fever had gone as quickly as it had come.

"We go home now? I don't like here," Chrissie fretted.

Neither do I, Amy thought, gathering her precious child into her arms. "Yes, my darling. We can go home now," she answered, elated that she was to be able to say that. "Get your dolly, and we will wait right here for Daddy to come back for us."

Amy, silently thanked God that they were at last safe, and that Chrissie had been spared from witnessing the bizarre and horrendous experiences that had taken place.

Suddenly, she realized that miraculously Chrissie had gone to sleep only a few moments before the appearance of the mysterious creatures, and awakened immediately after they had left. She wondered if somehow that this had been part of their plan. But, she had no idea what that plan was.

Satisfied that everything had returned to normalcy, Matthew rushed to their sides and announced with intense relief, "The storm has passed. We can go. Let's go home." The words, "Let's go home", sounded like music to their ears.

Matthew placed a restraining hand on Amy's arm as she started for the door. "Amy, one thing...When we get back home, I insist you call your obstetrician right away. I am concerned about the baby's condition. With all you have been though, I'm worried if the both of you are really all right."

"Please don't worry about me. I'm fine now, and so is the baby."

"You don't know that for sure. I really would feel better if you would go see your doctor. I can't help worrying about the both of you."

"You worry too much, Matt, please relax. I know the baby is all right. Just call it a mother's intuition. I assure you we are going to have a fine healthy baby and, if my intuition is correct, it's going to be a boy."

Matthew's eyes widened as he asked, "A boy, heh?"

A flash of humor crossing her face, Amy smiled teasingly as she added, "Yes. After all, that is what I ordered for you."

"A boy would be great. And I love you, but I'm still worried about you. Please humor me, Amy."

"We are all right, Matt, but if it will make you feel better, I'll go to the doctor's office soon for a checkup. You will see that everything is fine. Now, can we please go home?"

"Make it tomorrow," Matthew firmly insisted.

"Okay, okay, I'll go. Let's go home," Amy said, anxious to get out of that place that had been their prison for what seemed like a lifetime.

Matthew quickly extinguished the kerosene lanterns and lifted Chrissie into his arms, along with her doll and blanket. Touching Amy's elbow, he protectively urged her toward the door. Thinking how wonderful it felt to be free to go home at last, Matthew stopped hesitantly at the door and cast his eyes about searching for any indications of further danger. Seeing nothing abnormal, he breathed a sigh of relief.

Amy, close at his heels, paused and turned for a final gaze at the room that she was elated to leave. She had never thought she would be as happy to be going home as she was at that moment.

Looking about carefully for any signs of their earlier captors returning, Matthew and Amy stepped out into the twilight, each pausing to inhale the fresh clean air that they had never fully appreciated until then.

Wading through the tall grasses toward the road, they each couldn't help being apprehensive about the green creatures. Amy and Matthew still didn't know why they had appeared, and why they left as quickly as they did. But for now, the family was glad to finally be able to return home. There would be time enough later to sort out the mystery of what had happened within these last few hours...if it was at all possible.

Chapter 18

Among the lacy cirrus clouds sweeping over the horizon were the first sparkling stars making their appearance in the cobalt and golden sky of the late summer evening.

This being his favorite time of day, Harry Deakins rested his arm on the open window of his pickup truck as he leisurely drove down the country road. Inhaling the clean country air that was already beginning to cool with the coming night, he marveled at the awesome spectacle of the colorful sunset, which was reflecting all the colors of the rainbow.

En route back to Spring Hill from a business trip to Topeka, Harry decided to check on Lizzie Thornton before he returned to his office to check his messages and collect his mail before calling it quits for the day.

Checking often on Lizzie was his excuse of being able to see the woman that had stolen his heart many years ago. He hoped that in time she would heal from her heartache and would be able to go on with her life, which he hoped would include him. He vowed that he would wait for her no matter how long it would take.

Humming a happy and giddy tune, Harry was deep in thought as he reflected about the successful day he had. Thoughts of Lizzie, however, kept intruding in his mind, as he cruised in the direction toward her house.

Absorbed in his musings, he almost missed seeing the stranded vehicle along the roadside as he drove past.

"Why, that's the McCormack's car," Harry proclaimed aloud as he pressed his foot hard on the brakes, and quickly pulled over to the shoulder of the road. "Oh, my gosh. I hope nobody's been hurt."

Leaping out of the truck, he ran back to the stranded vehicle which was sitting at a perilously pitched angle with its right front wheel hanging in mid-air. He anxiously peered inside half dreading what he might find. Relieved to find that there was no one inside, Harry looked around for the McCormacks' whereabouts. He thought that maybe they might already be safe at home, yet, on the other hand...

Harry ambled around with his eyes to the ground, wondering about their whereabouts. He stepped to the front of the vehicle and searched the surroundings for any clues. The sun was swiftly disappearing from the horizon. He knew that it would soon be too dark to find them if they were still there in the remote area. Also, they may possibly be injured and needed help.

Stepping forward, Harry stopped when his boot crunched upon something underfoot. He looked down to see what appeared to be a gold object lying on the ground glimmering dimly from the remaining glow of the setting sunlight. Stooping to pick up the object, he found it to be a child's hair barrette embellished with a tiny pink rosette.

"Say...This has to be the little girl's hair clasp. I think I've seen her wearin' it. That means they must have gone that-a-way," Harry said aloud, frowning with speculation about their whereabouts.

His brow furrowing, he absent-mindedly fingered the hair ornament as he looked up the road. It did not make sense to him as why they would have gone in the opposite direction from their home. The not knowing of the McCormacks' whereabouts was becoming more alarming all the while to the old-timer.

"Hey, anybody out there?" he yelled distraughtly, scanning the area. "Yoo-hoo, is anybody there?" Harry continued calling out as he started up the road searching for them.

It was getting dark, causing it to be more difficult to see in the duskiness, but he didn't wish to abandon his search for the missing family. Frantic with worry, he continued calling their names in the hope of finding them safe and sound, pausing often to listen for a response to his calls. All he heard, however, was an unseen night owl hooting from the distance. His mouth dipped into an even deeper frown.

After a while, his search fruitless, he was about to abandon his search and return to his truck when he detected a movement a few yards ahead. Straining his eyes, he could barely make out the dark image of a couple approaching from the direction of the old abandoned storage building. They were wading through the scrub-brush and tall grass as they slowly made their way to the road.

"Helloo...That you, McCormack?" Harry called out in hope that it was the missing family. Scrambling toward the figures approaching from the direction of the old abandoned building, he was curious as to why anyone would have been at that old building at this time of day.

"Yes, Mr. Deakins, it's us," Matthew called to the elderly gentlemen, as the young family drew nearer.

Heaving a sigh of relief to find that it was the McCormacks, Harry excitedly began speaking loudly over the remaining distance, not waiting until they were within speaking distance. He was much too anxious to find out the details as to what had happened.

"I'm sure glad to see you. I saw your car back there, 'n' I wondered what had happened to you folks. You okay, 'n' how's the young'un?"

"Yes, Mr. Deakins, we are fine. We're glad to see you, too," Matthew answered, as the exhausted family drew nearer to the anxiously awaiting man. Matthew and Amy were relieved and grateful to be among normal human beings at last.

"What happened...'n' what were you doin' up there at that old buildin'?"

"We were on our way to..." Matthew breathlessly began to answer, setting Chrissie down on her feet, and handing the blanket to Amy.

He refrained from saying more after he and Amy quickly exchanged glances, long enough to convey between them an unspoken agreement. They both realized it would be best not to relate what they had just gone through, for who in their right mind would ever believe the bizarre story they would have been told?

Caught up in his excitement in finding the McCormacks all right, it didn't occur to Harry that Matthew didn't answer his questions. Instead, he rambled on, not giving the young couple a chance to get a word in edgewise, "I was jus' on the way to check on Lizzie when I saw your car over there on the side of the road. I knew it had to be yours. There's not 'nother'un like it here 'bouts."

Chuckling to himself with giddiness, he thought of the foolishness of anyone owning a convertible, a Mercedes besides, on a farm in Kansas. It was a far cry from pickups and tractors, and impractical for this lifestyle.

Seriously, he added, "I was 'fraid you were hurt, or somethin'. You sure you're okay?"

"Yes, we are fine...only a bit shaken up. We just want to get home," Amy answered while Harry worriedly looked from her to Matthew.

"Say, that's a nasty ole' bump you've got there on your head, McCormack. You sure you're okay, 'n' what about the rest of you? Maybe I should take you in to the doctor to look you over," the concerned gentleman said, observing them closely for further injuries.

"No, I'm fine. I just hit my head on something. It's nothing to worry about. I'll be okay. We are just anxious to get home, and we need to get Chrissie to bed," Matthew said, in hopes that the gentleman didn't question them further.

Harry, unable to refrain from thinking about their recklessness, said to himself, "Yep, them young city kids; they drive too damn fast. They never learn 'till it's too late. A senseless shame to have the babe with them 'sides. Don't they know their little'un could've been killed? Yep, it's a senseless shame. Anyways, they're lucky it wasn't worse."

A severe headache forming, reminded Matthew of the injury to his head, making it a painful reality. As he tentatively touched his forehead, he found that the wound had stopped bleeding except for a few drops of blood appearing on the surface. A dry crust on the painful lump was already forming.

Remaining quiet, Amy stood nearby on numb shaking legs, absentmindedly clutching Chrissie's blue blanket to her body as if she was protectively holding her child. She had no feeling within her shocked body, only the weak numbness that refused to go away. Her head spun in dizziness as she thought about the tormenting experience they had just lived through, and of the mysterious green creatures that had held them captive.

The conversation between the two men drifted in and out through Amy's hazy mind as if from a far distance. She wondered if what had happened to them had really occurred, or whether it only had been an awful nightmare. In her dazed mind, she wondered if she had only dreamed that they had been chased by a terrible storm cloud.

Was it a dream that they had been in an accident? The old and dank building--the mysterious green beings--Did it really occur? But, she realized it had to have happened, for they were standing in the middle of the road at nightfall with Harry Deakins, and Matthew had been hurt--His head was bleeding.

Satisfied that the family was all right, Harry offered, "Pickup's back there. Come on, 'n' I'll take you home first, 'fore I'll go on over to Lizzie's. I was on my way over there when I saw your car."

"Thank you, Mr. Deakins. We are thankful that you came along when you did," Matthew said in gratitude that Harry had arrived on the scene when he had, as they were extremely exhausted from their long horrific ordeal.

Scooping Chrissie up into his arms, Matthew ushered Amy toward the truck which was parked a few feet down the road. He was aware that it would be useless to try to move their vehicle until the next morning when it would be light.

Hesitating, Amy looked back over her shoulder and gazed back toward the building where their nightmare had ended. She was unable to see the building now for the evening was quickly turning into the darkness of night. The darkness made Amy feel the bizarre nightmare they had just endured a short time ago was of another lifetime.

A cold chill went down her spine. There were many questions still left unanswered. Who were those creatures? What were they, and from where did they come? And why?

She only knew that the mysterious green beings would have had to come with the storm. She couldn't shake the feeling that these creatures were sent to warn them--and to protect them. But, from what? It was all much too baffling.

Those unbelievable creatures were so threatening and vicious. Yet, suddenly they had become gentle, their eyes filled with compassion. Those eyes...Amy thought that she will not ever be able to forget those huge, dark eyes.

Harry in his excitement continued with his one-sided chatter. "Good thin' I was runnin' late this evenin'. I 'most decided not to come out. Had to go into Topeka 'n' was jus' gettin' back. Didn't even go into the office yet. Thought I should come by Lizzie's first 'fore headin' into town," he said, shaking his head. "Good thin' though that I did." The elderly man thought about what could have happened if they had been injured--or worse.

Upon reaching the truck which was parked alongside the road, Matthew helped Amy and Chrissie into the cab. Then, he gently squeezed Amy's arm in assurance that their nightmare was over, and they could relax.

"We're going home, Amy. Everything will be all right now."

Remaining silent, she could only respond with a quivering weak smile. Settling back against the warm leather seat, Amy wondered if their lives would, or could, ever be the same again, and whether they would ever be able to put this nightmare behind them.

It entered her mind, however, that the ordeal they had survived through brought her and her husband closer together than ever before. She was positive that after what they had endured they would now be able to overcome any obstacle that they might encounter in the future.

Getting into the truck alongside Amy and firmly shutting the door, Matthew leaned across Amy and Chrissie to ask Harry, "Did it rain much your way? Was there any storm damage around here? The way the clouds looked, it must have been a pretty bad storm."

The older man cast a quick puzzling glance at Matthew. Contemplating what Matthew had just said, he gazed out the window.

Removing his gray Stetson hat from his head and laying it upon the corner of the dash, he ran his fingers slowly through his thinning gray hair as he scanned the sky that was filling with bright stars.

"What rain? Storm, you say?" Shrugging, he glanced at Matthew, his brow pulling into a bewildered frown. "Don't know 'bout any rain here 'bouts. Doesn't look like we've got any here. Everythin's dry."

Biting his lips in puzzlement, Harry stared out at the terrain as they passed by. It didn't look as if it had rained, nor had there been rain in the forecast. He had been listening to the car radio most of the time to and from Topeka, and nothing had been mentioned about the probability of storms, or that it had stormed. Much less, anything regarding the much-needed rain.

"That's strange. I would have thought sure..." Matthew said, knitting his eyebrows in question.

Worried about Matthew's confusion, Harry stroked his chin as he studied his face, and thought that the blow to his head really must have gotten to him. He wasn't making sense. Making the decision, however, to keep his thoughts to himself, Harry drawled on, "We sure do need a good rain, though. Hadn't had a real good soaker in 'while now. If it did rain any, it sure wasn't 'nough to settle the dust. But," he said with a sigh, "I've been in Topeka most of the day, so maybe I'm wrong..."

Becoming fidgety, Chrissie squirmed around between the confines of her parent's legs, not liking to be kept immobile between her parents. She wiggled around until the radio on the dash drew her attention. Beaming happily, she quickly reached out with her chubby little hand to turn the knob on. When Amy saw what Chrissie was about to do, she immediately stopped her.

Amused, Harry chuckled good-naturedly as he insisted, "Hey, that's okay. Let her switch it on. I don't mind a bit." He smiled and winked at Chrissie as he said, "Go 'head, Cutie-pie. How 'bout some good ole' country music? Find us somethin' real good to listen to."

Elated that he had given his permission, Chrissie's eyes sparkled as she switched on the radio. A country song was droning away. She leaned back contentedly against her mother as they continued their journey homeward.

Harry hummed along with the tune, while Amy and Matthew were silent, each lost in their thoughts, as they passed the widow Thornton's homestead, where a yellowish glow from a lamp lit the windows of the forlorn house.

It was when Harry slowed the pickup to turn into the long driveway that led to the McCormack's house that the three adults suddenly sat up fully alerted. Each of the occupants strained forward to see more clearly. Each gasped.

"What is that light?" Amy shrieked.

"Damned if I know."

"What's goin' on here?"

"I can't believe it!" Matthew exclaimed.

"NOoooooo ..." Amy moaned, as they stared at the unbelievable sight before them. "Tell me it's not so."

As they drew nearer, the lights ahead became brighter, intermingling with orange and black hues, as they lightened the darkening sky. There was fire, bright orange raging flames leaping upward, and the smoke was intense with ugly black plumes coiling skyward like a giant tornado.

Besides the glow from the fire, there were other lights visible...bright searchlights, lights from the television crews, and flashing red emergency lights. People were milling around everywhere, from firefighters trying to contain the huge fire to police cars, ambulances, and television crews, circling around the site of the fire. Spectators were looking on in wonder.

Among them was Lizzie Thornton nervously twisting the hem of her apron with her shaking hands.

Where the white two-story house had stood was with its welcoming wraparound veranda with cascading roses climbing lavishly over the white railing, and the red barn and corrals--everything was gone. Remaining was a giant sunken pit of fire, smoke, and charred ruin. Around the perimeter, all living things, also, lay in ruin. Smoking patches of burnt grass were evident, while new hotspots kept forming from the never-dying sparks being carried in the hot breeze.

Harry brought the truck to a sudden halt. The occupants could not move, nor could they speak. They could only stare in silent disbelief and shock. The music coming from the radio stopped, as if it, too, was in a trance.

A newscaster's voice came over the airwaves, breaking the silence as he announced,

> "This is Richard Adams from WNG news, reporting live from the location of a horrifying disaster caused by what appears to have been a giant meteorite. Firefighters and emergency crews from several communities are successfully containing the huge fire which has completely destroyed this rural home. It had been feared that the occupants hadn't been able to escape this catastrophe. It, however, has been reported by Lizzie Thornton, a neighbor of the McCormacks, that she had seen the occupants, Matthew and Amy McCormack, with their small daughter, Chrissie, leaving shortly before the tragedy had occurred."

The news-caster's voice repeated the bulletin as the truck occupants continued to sit in shocked silence hearing only glimpses.

"...home...a large meteorite...

...Lizzie Thornton...

...left moments before...

...a <u>miracle</u> that they..."

EPILOGUE

Kneeling on the plush green grass in her front yard, Amy McCormack tended to her rosebushes, a task she loved doing. Humming contentedly while she worked, she thought about how gloriously happy she was, happier than she had ever thought possible.

Nearby on the lawn, was a patchwork quilt with a small child sitting upon it. He was gurgling, happily absorbed in his own little world, playing with the assortment of toys that were strewn about upon the quilt.

Nathan was a beautiful, healthy, and robust child. His angelic face was framed with bouncing soft curls, the color of field-ripened wheat. In time, his hair would darken to be like his father's, and his footsteps would follow his proud father, something his father had looked forward to and dreamed of for a long while.

His eyes--those huge doe-like dark eyes--tugged on anyone's heartstrings. Nathan couldn't speak yet, but he didn't have to. His eyes told all, as they would change with his every mood. A bright sparkle reflecting in his eyes radiated his excitement and happiness, only changing to an endless depth of black intensity when he was unhappy.

When he was extremely displeased, which was rare, his eyes would blaze like hot coals. It had often occurred to Amy that no one in either Matthew's or in her family had eyes of that color, which made her often wonder.

Looking into the child's dark eyes whenever he was in that particular dark mood, it always reminded her of that one awful summer evening almost two years before...the one that started out as a glorious day and ended in horror. The day that had changed all their lives forever.

Never would she forget the terrible storm...and the terrorizing green ghostlike creatures that came with it...the creatures that ultimately saved their lives. <u>His</u> eyes....

The small boy's eyes, reflecting a soft tenderness, radiated pure innocence with a warm inner glow of wonder and contentment, as well as love and trust.

His petite blonde sister, Chrissie, was on the front porch playing tea party with her dolls. One of which remained the small girl's favorite companion--a threadbare rag doll with fraying yellow yarn hair and fading painted features. Like her baby brother, the charming girl was a picture of health and vitality. Her fair skin was aglow, and her cheeks were rosy from the fresh country air. Whoever saw Chrissie was always enchanted by her loveliness.

"Mommy, look. Someone is coming," Chrissie called to her mother when she noticed someone walking up the long drive. The four-year-old girl eagerly rose to her feet to see who their visitor might be. The approaching figure, however, was much too far away to be recognizable.

Pausing at her work, Amy straightened to see whom Chrissie saw. Watching the lone figure slowly approach, Amy instantly recognized their visitor. Smiling at her daughter's excitement, she watched as the figure passed by the large farm pond alongside the drive.

Another farmhouse had once stood where the pond was now, a few cattle quenching their thirst along the shallow edge of the water, while others were grazing nearby.

Amy's attention turned to Chrissie's black and white spotted dog yelping excitedly at something in the grass near where the cattle were grazing. It was perhaps a brown terrapin, too stubborn, or too frightened, to move. Amy smiled. Such simple and common everyday events as this still amazed and delighted her.

As the figure draw nearer, Chrissie began to shout joyously when she finally recognized the woman that was approaching. It was unmistakably their neighbor, Lizzie Thornton.

Lizzie was easily recognizable from what she was wearing, her white freshly laundered and starched bibbed apron over a multicolored print cotton dress. She wore a white sunbonnet over her nearly gray hair that she had neatly arranged in a low bun at the base of her head.

"Mommy, it's Aunt Lizzie," Chrissie announced ecstatically, abandoning her tea party. "Aunt Lizzie is coming, Aunt Lizzie is coming," Chrissie chanted, jumping up and down jubilantly.

"Why, so it is," Amy, smiling, answered in a tone of mocked surprise, pretending she hadn't known the identity of the person coming up their drive. She, herself, was pleased to see the elderly woman approach. Laying down her tools, Amy rose to her feet as she watched her neighbor walk up the long driveway. Being secluded out in the open country, with Lizzie being her nearest neighbor, Amy always welcomed her visits.

The friendship between the two women had come a long way since the time when Amy and Matthew purchased the farm estate. Neither woman had anticipated that they would form a warm and close relationship between them, until the McCormacks' tragedy brought them together.

The woman ambling up the road was unmindful of the puffs of dust swirling about her feet. Moving at a slow pace as only her age allowed, she paused now and then to emit a slight gasp of awe, as she enjoyed the panoramic view surrounding her. She looked up at the brilliant blue sky and saw a few white cumulus clouds mushrooming in the far horizon. She thought it might rain before the day ended. A nice spring rain would be welcomed to settle the dust.

Lizzie's heart quickened as she approached nearer to the beautiful and welcoming traditional country house that sat upon a slight incline, surrounded by a white rail fence that enclosed a breathtaking yard that reflected Amy's loving care.

Always reminded of the disastrous event that occurred almost two years ago, Lizzie thought how courageous Amy and Matthew were in not giving up.

Ahead, beyond the house, Lizzie could see the red hay barn, more contemporary in structure than the one that had been there before, and new corrals. There were, also, other new buildings. Among them was a smaller replica of the old cylinder grain silo that had once been there, standing tall in contrast to the other rectangular buildings. There were still a few remnants remaining from the disaster that would soon be gone.

She could clearly see the hard work the McCormacks had done in replacing all they had lost. The love they had put into it was clearly visible.

Chrissie, jumping up and down in excitement, bounded down the porch steps to meet the woman who had become like a member of their own family.

"Hi, Aunt Lizzie, I knew it was you. I saw you coming. I'm so glad you came. Come, have some tea with us."

Chrissie motioned to the miniature table with tiny cups and

saucers set upon it. Surrounding the table were matching miniature chairs filled with her favorite dolls and stuffed animals.

"In a little while, Honey, Lizzie answered, laughing in amusement when she saw the multitude of toys occupying the tiny chairs.

Amy smiled brightly at the woman that was now coming through the gate. She brushed aside a stray blond tendril from her damp forehead without thought, leaving a dirty smudge upon her brow, as she waved to her friend in welcome.

Matthew and Amy's acceptance of the woman came about that fateful day which changed their lives, and turned Lizzie's life around. It was then that Lizzie had at last come face to face with reality and was able to overcome the grief from the loss of her precious family.

Even though her family was never far from her thoughts, Lizzie no longer mourned for them. She had finally accepted the fact that her husband and daughter were gone, and that she would have to go on with her life without them. Now, Amy and Matthew, with their children, Chrissie and Nathan, were her family. She cherished them as if they were her own.

Lizzie realized that she had only existed until that fateful day, almost two years ago, when she had awakened to life, and found that she still cared--not so much for herself--but for others. Her new neighbors had tried to befriend her, but in return, she had refused to reciprocate their friendship. Until she found the McCormack family in trouble, she didn't want to be bothered. Lizzie couldn't have cared less until she had realized they needed her help, then her goodness from within replaced her self-pity.

Lizzie was awakened to the fact that not only did the McCormacks have good intentions toward her, but also Harry, her lifelong friend. He had always been there for her, always ready to lend a helping hand. And his consideration and admiration has not ceased.

She knew she was fortunate--very fortunate indeed. She, at long last, felt truly blessed to have such friends.

Before Amy could voice a welcome to their visitor, Chrissie

ran to Lizzie. Enthusiastically throwing her small arms around the frail woman's legs, she nearly knocked the elderly woman off her balance.

"Aunt Lizzie, did you bring me something?" Chrissie asked as she bounced around eagerly, knowing fully well that Aunt Lizzie never came visiting empty-handed.

Lizzie always had ready a surprise for the children. It didn't matter what the surprise would be, whether it be large or small, the children were always delighted. It always brought Lizzie much joy to see the children's eager anticipation of what she brought.

"Here, Child, I picked these just for you. Beautiful flowers for a beautiful little girl," Lizzie said, her face beaming with a loving expression, as she held out a large bunch of fragrant spring flowers she had gathered from her flower beds.

Caught up in Chrissie's exuberance, the small boy wouldn't be outdone by his big sister. He pushed himself up on all four limbs before he awkwardly stood on his tottering chubby legs. He warbled words in his own unintelligible baby language. His huge dark eyes were bright with recognition as he wobbled off the quilt and tottered clumsily toward the old woman.

Amy started to reach out for the toddler before he should stumble and fall, but chose to not intervene when she saw the joy written on the elderly woman's face.

Lizzie quickly set down the cloth-covered wicker basket she carried, the aroma of freshly baked bread from within drifted through the air. She stooped down to the boy's level in delight as he collapsed into her arms.

"That's my boy. How is my precious, precious Nathan?" Lizzie crooned, her face all-aglow.

The child worked his small mouth, trying his hardest to speak. A tiny frown appeared on his brow before his eyes softened in sudden recognition of what he wanted to say.

"Wuv 'ou. Wuv 'ou, Wizzie," little Nathan said, the precious words tumbling from his pink lips. In a swift motion, he planted a big wet, sloppy kiss on Lizzie's cheek.

Watching the scene unfold in front of her, Amy swallowed hard, as tears of emotion blurred her eyes. Trying to contain her tears, she turned her gaze away toward the side yard a few feet from the house where Matthew was busy repairing his tractor.

Matthew was eager to get back to his spring plowing. There was much he wanted, and needed, to do. Pausing a moment to wipe his sweating brow, he glanced up to see Amy gazing his way.

Their simultaneous smiles met in mutual understanding, as they remembered their dream, as they always would...the dream that they had shared--and almost lost. Through their dedicated love for each other, and perseverance, that dream was now theirs forever.

Noticing Lizzie's presence with his family, Matthew laid down his tools and quickly joined them, already mischievously making his plans to tease the poor woman.

Impishly, he smiled, knowing without a doubt that he would bring a blush to Lizzie's face, as he asked, "How's that fellow... what's his name? Oh, yeah...Harry. I haven't seen him in awhile, but I guess he's been kept pretty busy lately by someone, right?"

Of course, Lizzie blushed. "He is just fine and dandy. In fact, he's coming to supper tonight. I will tell him you asked about him if you would like," she replied, trying hard to suppress a giggle.

Picking up the covered basket she had brought, she handed it to Amy. "I've baked fresh bread. Harry always likes my homemade bread, so I baked him some. I have an extra loaf for you folks; it's still warm. There's a jar of jam in here, too."

"Thank you, Lizzie, for your thoughtfulness. Don't mind Matt. You know he loves to tease you," Amy said laughingly as she accepted the wicker basket from Lizzie and inhaled the delectable aroma. "This bread looks and smells wonderful."

"You are welcome and I hope you enjoy it. Well, I had better get back home and start on supper," Lizzie said. Turning toward Matthew with a smug smile, she added, "That fellow...I think his name is Harry...will be here soon to eat."

Matthew, encircling his arm lovingly around Amy's shoulder,

wasn't going to let Lizzie go without a final comment. Grinning wickedly, he asked, "Seems like old Harry is coming over for supper quite a bit lately, isn't he? Has he forgotten how to cook for himself, or is there some other reason I don't know about?"

Amy elbowed him in the side for the banter, thinking he was going a bit overboard with his teasing.

Lizzie didn't answer. She didn't have to. Smiling smugly, she gave each child a loving hug and kiss before she turned and started out the gate. Closing the gate behind her, she smiled as she raised her arm and waved back to the McCormack family.

Waving in return, Amy and Matthew and watched Lizzie saunter slowly down their drive, dust rising once again at her shuffling feet.

Both were silent as they each reflected about what their life had become. They had come close to losing everything that was important to them, including their dream. Even through misfortune, they had held onto that dream, and through it all, they had found much, much more.

Without a doubt, Matthew and Amy McCormack knew their dream, as well as their love, had been worth fighting for. As a result of their love and determination, their lives couldn't be more complete--or more perfect.

Can it last? Ask Amy.

She will be quick to answer, "Oh, yes. As long as we have each other and our love...and, yes--our dreams--we will prevail."

The End

Made in the USA
Columbia, SC
06 March 2021